Forever
Is a
LIE

A Thing beyond Forever
That Kiss in the Rain
How About a Sin Tonight?
Ex
Black Suits You

Stranger Trilogy
Marry Me, Stranger
All Yours, Stranger
Forget Me Not, Stranger

Forever
Is a
LIE

NOVONEEL
CHAKRABORTY

EBURY
PRESS

An imprint of Penguin Random House

EBURY PRESS

USA | Canada | UK | Ireland | Australia
New Zealand | India | South Africa | China

Ebury Press is part of the Penguin Random House group of companies
whose addresses can be found at global.penguinrandomhouse.com

Published by Penguin Random House India Pvt. Ltd
7th Floor, Infinity Tower C, DLF Cyber City,
Gurgaon 122 002, Haryana, India

First published in Ebury Press by Penguin Random House India 2017

Copyright © Novoneel Chakraborty 2017

10 9 8 7 6 5

ISBN 9780143427490

Typeset in Requiem Text by Manipal Digital Systems, Manipal
Printed at Thomson Press India Ltd, New Delhi

www.penguin.co.in

For Al Eye, AP and Whoosh

On the Eve of His Twenty-Eighth Birthday

9 November 2010

He looks at the arrangement on the terrace of a forty-floor high-rise in Mumbai. A cosy mattress, a transparent tent and five love candles around it. He heaves a sigh of satisfaction. He recently bought the terrace and the floor below it without telling her about it. Tonight he will turn one of her fantasies into reality. They will make love under the stars. Tonight he will also realize his five-year-old dream. He will ask her to marry him the moment the clock strikes twelve—on the eve of his twenty-eighth birthday. He has never been happier.

She is attending a corporate training programme, which is due to end in an hour, at a resort in Lonavla. She has checked her watch at least ten times in the last five minutes. Time seems not to be at its usual pace today. She does a quick mental math for the umpteenth time. Five more minutes for the training session to get over, two minutes to greet everyone, say goodbye, another two minutes to hit the highway and then a couple of hours to reach Mumbai if there's no untoward traffic. She has already asked her friend, an expert at baking, to make his favourite: blueberry cheesecake. She will make a detour after she reaches Mumbai to collect the cake, which will not take more than half an hour. She will reach his place by 10 p.m. Good, she tells herself and checks her watch yet another time.

The tent is right in the middle of the terrace. He places the smooth white mattress inside and puts a soft blanket over it. The air has just the right amount of chill, which makes him crave for her. For a moment, he can almost see the two of them becoming one inside the tent. He snaps out of the tempting reverie and readjusts the position of the candles. Tonight should be the perfect night, the kind lovers fantasize about, or so he has in mind. He places a sixth candle, a fake one, right above the mattress, where they will place their heads. It is actually a candle-shaped box and has a diamond ring inside.

She feels elated to hear the final 'thank you for being such a nice batch' from the trainer. The session is officially over for the day. She rushes out, greeting whomever she meets on her way. Almost everyone asks her if she wants to accompany them to Lion's Point, a famous mountaintop, but she politely says no and calls her driver.

Satisfied with the preparation on the terrace, he makes his way to the flat and heads straight into the kitchen. He had googled and written down the recipe of sun-dried tomato risotto, her favourite, on a

Post-it note. He has also arranged for Montoya Cabernet Sauvignon—one of the best red wines in the world—as the perfect accompaniment. Suddenly he wants to hear her voice and decides to call her.

She is in the car now. She picks up her phone to call him and finds him calling her. This is how synchronized they are in their relationship. Be it matters of the heart or the mind, they are always on the same page. And it's this very perfect timing that has gently pushed them into seeking a forever together every day. She says a soft hello into the phone.

He talks to her for some time and then lies that he has some important official work to complete. He has never been the kind who would surprise anybody, but this time he wants everything to be special, a memory that would last forever. She believes his lie. He cuts the call and wears an apron.

She hums her favourite romantic song while checking the photo gallery of her phone. Her car climbs the treacherous roads of Lonavla, with hills on one side and a gorge on the other. A boulder is displaced a few feet above the road that her car is on. Tearing the safety net around the boulders, placed to stop them from sliding down abruptly, it falls exactly on top of her car. It crushes the vehicle out of shape and the driver and her out of recognition. Her heartbeat stops almost immediately.

He keeps waiting to surprise her.

1

Five years, seven months and twenty-one days later

Name: Prisha Srivastav
Age: Eighteen
Sex: Female
Occupation: Student

This was her profile information on Facebook. Ditto on Tinder, a dating app. With moist eyes, she checked the *about me* section on the app, which she had just filled up:

I'm here to hook up for a night. Anyone who wants anything that goes beyond a night, please swipe left.

Prisha forced herself not to think as she started browsing through men's profiles on the app. Tinder was recommended to her by Zinnia, her roommate. Two years her senior in college, Zinnia was from the same neighbourhood as Prisha in Faridabad. She had shifted to Bengaluru to pursue media management from Cross University.

Prisha had followed in her footsteps and shifted to Bengaluru a month ago and had taken admission at the same university. She had enrolled herself as a BA student, with a major in mass communication. Zinnia and Prisha stayed together in a rented apartment on BTM Layout.

It was Zinnia who had first described Tinder as a saviour of singles in the city. But Prisha hadn't made an account on the dating site because she was single, but because she had been feeling emotionally violated for a few months now.

Anyone remotely good-looking and Prisha would swipe right. In fact, looks didn't matter at all for what she had in mind. She had heard about Tinder earlier from a number of friends but had never imagined using it one day. Why would she? She had been in a committed relationship since she had turned thirteen—until two months ago when she had stepped into her penultimate teenage year. In all these years there had been only one boy she was doggedly, single-mindedly and with utmost sincerity committed to.

Utkarsh Arora had wooed her for an entire summer vacation before she had finally said yes. She was in Class VII and he was in Class X. (Love, then, was an alien feeling. It slowly turned real as they gave it time). And just when Prisha had started believing that there could be no one better than Utkarsh, he let her down.

She had invited him to a family function. It was a dream to see her boyfriend enjoy with her family and cousins;

everyone had approved of him. Three weeks later, she had noticed that Utkarsh's Facebook relationship status had changed from: *in a relationship with Prisha Srivastav* to *in a relationship with Shelly Srivastav*. Shelly was her cousin and two years older than her. Prisha demanded an explanation but all Utkarsh said was that he was *now* in love with Shelly. Now? Is love a prisoner of time? Not only did Utkarsh not give her any plausible explanation, but he repeatedly dodged her calls and then blocked her on social media and on his phone. When she turned to Shelly for an answer, she simply said, 'He loves me, not you.'

At eighteen, when one's world collapses, it also brings down with it the beliefs one has grown up on. You stop trusting in truths altogether. You start believing that a truth is nothing but an illusion. Some call it the loss of innocence. It is then that people start giving in to the collective lies that makes everyone sorted adults. Prisha's attempt at creating a Tinder profile was proof enough that she had given in to it as well.

Love, Prisha concluded within a month of her break-up, was a fallacy. Lust was real; the body was real. And henceforth, she would get real too. Even if it meant living a life she didn't believe in.

Seven hours after she had made her Tinder profile, there were thirteen matches. When Zinnia came back from college, Prisha gave the phone to her.

'I think this dude looks cute. What do you think?' Zinnia said, looking at the fifth match. Prisha couldn't

3

care less. Zinnia chatted with the guy on Prisha's behalf and in no time fixed a date later in the night at Harry's in Koramangala. Zinnia knew Prisha's story, but she wasn't the one who had given her the idea of a one-night stand. It was something Prisha had inquired herself when Zinnia kept ranting about some guy who went by the name the 'Mean Monster' in the Bangalore party circuit. Mean because he was infamous for his edging technique—a method by which orgasm could be delayed, pushing the body to feel pleasure like never before. And monster because what he carried between his legs was two inches more than that of an average Indian's. Zinnia was more than excited when she was finally able to trace the elusive guy and pin him down for a date, coincidentally on the same night that Prisha was supposed to meet her Tinder date.

'You'll have to come with me, Zin,' Prisha said as soon as Zinnia had fixed the place for her to meet the Tinder guy.

'Of course! But I too have a date, sweets,' she said. Prisha noticed that Zinnia was blushing slightly, which was very unlike her.

'What?' Prisha asked, surprised.

'Finally I'm going to meet him tonight.'

'Who?'

'The Mean Monster.'

Prisha didn't really care much, but seeing her flatmate's excitement, she pretended otherwise.

'Don't worry, we are going to the same place,' Zinnia winked.

Hours later, the two girls were at Harry's, waiting for their dates. Though she was nervous, Prisha tried her best to remain poised, sipping her mojito. As she looked around anticipating the arrival of her date, Utkarsh's face kept flashing in front of her eyes. Although he had ditched her, she kept feeling as if her own promises had been false.

Don't drink so fast, Zinnia WhatsApped her. Prisha turned and gave her a forced smile.

And don't be pushy. Like, don't give the despo vibe. Let the guy take the lead. He should feel you are a prize—another message popped up from her.

Okay, Prisha responded.

Finally the Tinder guy, Niraj, appeared. Prisha felt her palms sweating. She shook hands with him. He took his seat and immediately got busy placing orders with the waiter. He first sat opposite her but after the waiter walked away, he came around to sit beside her. Prisha glanced at Zinnia, who gave her an encouraging smile, sipping her beer. Niraj started chatting casually and in between kept complimenting her on her physical features—her eyes, her hair, her lips. It was all okay, until he started getting close and would touch her on the slightest pretext. Prisha didn't know how to react. The music was loud and he kept leaning on her shoulder to speak into her ears. The way his breath touched her ears suddenly made her unsure of her decision to be there. She excused herself and quickly messaged Zinnia: *You please be there, okay? I'm not feeling good.*

Prisha waited impatiently for a response. There was none; her message was delivered, but Zinnia had not read it yet. She turned to look at where she was sitting but Zinnia wasn't there. There was a different couple sitting there instead. Prisha immediately waved at the waiter. 'Where did that girl go?' she asked, pointing towards the table where Zinnia was sitting.

'I'm sorry, but I'm not sure. You want me to ask my colleague who was serving the table?' the waiter said.

Prisha became thoughtful. 'It's okay,' she finally said.

'Anything wrong?' Niraj asked, when she looked back at him. She is an easy catch, he thought, and had his next moves neatly planned out. He would kiss her and if she didn't resist, the obvious proposal would follow. As he kept talking, looking for a pretext to kiss her, Prisha simply kept nodding, absent-minded, glancing at the table where Zinnia was sitting from time to time, wondering if the Monster—or whatever his name was—had already taken her.

2

'Should we go? Actually, the music is getting on my nerves now,' Niraj asked, knowing fully well that it was the lamest excuse of letting a girl know that enough with the chit-chat, it was now time for some action. He had already stripped Prisha off in his mind. And if she was even half of what he had imagined her to be, it would be a night to remember.

'Okay,' Prisha said softly, feeling her guts churn. If sitting and waiting for Niraj had made her question her decision to meet him, she was now certain of having made a mistake. Picking up men for casual sex wasn't her cup of tea. Her angst against Utkarsh had inflated her darker side a little too much for her own comfort. There is a difference between thinking something and actually doing it. Prisha had decided that she would turn into a girl who didn't give a fuck about who she slept with. But that idea now seemed far-fetched.

Prisha saw Niraj get up. He was done paying the bill. She too stood up, feeling her legs shake mildly. Should she tell him directly that she didn't want to prolong this discomfort of a date any more? Prisha wondered and followed him outside. She didn't like confrontations. Perhaps that's why Utkarsh had found it easier to avoid her. *Or to get rid of me,* she thought, *as if I were some tumour*. During the course of their relationship, she had never asked him any questions about anything. But when she did, he chose not to answer.

It was noisy outside as people queued up to go inside the pub. Prisha tried to talk to Niraj, but he was a few steps ahead of her. She walked faster but caught up with him only when he reached his car. They were in the parking lot, on the opposite side of the road, and Niraj immediately climbed in to the driver's seat, and waited for Prisha to join him. When she didn't, he rolled down the window and said, 'The door is unlocked.'

Unsure of what she was doing, Prisha finally opened the door and sat inside. She was about to say something when she felt his hand on her leg and his lips ready to clamp on hers. She stopped him instinctively, with her palm pressed against his mouth.

'I need to pee,' she said, quickly getting out of the car. Prisha was still uncertain of how to tell him that she didn't want to take this forward. 'I'll be waiting here,' Niraj said. She nodded and walked back to the pub. She then booked a cab from her phone, which was two minutes from her location but luckily, it arrived within a minute. Prisha waited at the exit. The moment she saw the cab, she quickly stepped out and got inside.

The driver took a U-turn and she ducked to stay out of Niraj's sight as the cab drove past his car. Once the cab was on the main road, Prisha deleted Tinder from her phone. She was happy to have not shared her number with her 'match'. This night had been a mistake. Just like those days and nights with Utkarsh.

When the person you have been with turns out to be wrong then do the realizations the person made you stumble upon stand as wrong too? If the relationship was a farce then what about those elements which you discovered within the farce? Can they be real? What do you do when the picture is fake but the colours in it are genuine? Prisha felt a lump in her throat. She didn't want to cry but the tears fought their way through from deep within. The person leaves, the realizations don't. Every second the realizations keep rooting themselves deeper and deeper until you crack open. And within that crack some disappear and some discover a new self. And survive.

The cabbie noticed her crying in the rear-view mirror and offered her some water. She refused politely and wiped her eyes. Soon the cab reached her apartment. Prisha went up and opened the main door with her set of keys. It was then that she heard Zinnia's moans. She had heard women moaning this loudly before, while watching porn videos with Utkarsh, but to hear it in reality made her feel a little awkward. She gently closed the door behind her. The way Zinnia was begging to be pleasured made Prisha uncomfortable; she could almost see her. Keeping the living room lights off, she plugged in her earphones and tapped on the music app. She then settled on a beanbag and played her favourite playlist. The music drowned out the moans but flooded her with memories of her emotional ruin. It was only when the playlist had ended that she opened her eyes. She glanced at the clock on her phone: 1.44 a.m. She pulled the earphones out. The house was silent. There was only a sliver of streetlight streaming into the flat. As her eyes adjusted to the darkness, she noticed a figure standing near the living room door, leaning against the wall. She looked at the silhouette; the man seemed muscular; he was only in his briefs. He was smoking. Prisha couldn't see much of his face except for his jawline. She could make out that he was looking at her.

'Do you want to say something?' Prisha asked, puncturing the awkward silence.

'What has happened?' the man asked. His voice was heavy; the kind that stays with you. The kind that sounds important, slightly reserved, as if he didn't talk much. She also guessed that he was perhaps not very young.

'What?' Prisha wasn't sure what was he talking about.

'You were crying.'

She held her gaze and shook her head.

'Nothing.'

'Heartbreak?' he asked instantly.

'How do you . . . you don't know me,' she spluttered.

'I know those tears,' he said. Prisha sighed. Running her fingers through her hair, she looked away from him.

After a thoughtful pause, she said, 'If you know the tears, would you know how to stop them?'

There was silence. The man took a long puff of his cigarette. 'What's your age?' he asked, exhaling the smoke.

'Eighteen. Why?'

She sensed a smirk.

'Just get this straight: Forever is a lie,' he said. And before Prisha could ask him anything else, he went back inside the bedroom, closing the door softly behind him. In no time, he was back in the living room, this time dressed in jeans and a T-shirt. The cigarette wasn't there either.

'Listen, I wanted to . . .' she began only to be cut short by the thud of the main door closing in response. Half a minute later she heard a bike ride off in full speed.

This man had to be the Mean Monster, Prisha thought to herself.

3

The bike stopped in front of a duplex at Indira Nagar. The man got down and unlocked the main door and stopped. The door had his name on it:

SAVEER RATHOD.

The nameplate was a thick golden structure with a black border. She chose the font on it, much like everything else in the duplex. In fact, it was supposed to have another name—her's—above his. *Supposed to have . . .* Before the past could shackle him again, Saveer walked inside.

Sensors in the house detected his movement and the rooms flooded with light as he made his way from the hall downstairs to the bedroom upstairs. The lights went out every time he exited a room. He had always wondered if he could do the same with his life. If, with every step forward, darkness could conceal his past like it had never been there. But life was different. It highlighted the past using the most powerful light source: memory. And in the dark alleys of one's memory, every bit of the past was pronounced. Especially the parts you desperately wanted to suppress.

The interior of the duplex was designed exactly the way she had told him once: glass ceilings, ground-level furniture, sensor lighting and plenty of potted plants. However, there was one object that he had intentionally avoided: mirrors. She had told him there would be a lot of mirrors in their duplex. She had always wanted to relish their reflection when they were together. And now Saveer couldn't look into a mirror for the same reason. Loneliness mocked at him when he saw his reflection. He didn't remember the last time he had looked into one. Even at salons, he would sit with his eyes closed and get up immediately after he was done. Reflections scared him, unsettled him and probed at a certain truth of his life, which he was yet to come to terms with.

As he started climbing the stairs to his bedroom, he stopped to glance at the adjacent wall. There were several framed photographs of her. He had deliberately kept her pictures to remind himself that perhaps he had never deserved the togetherness she had brought with her. Before the pictures could suck him inside a time machine potent enough to destroy whatever was left of him, Saveer dashed upstairs.

Once in his room, Saveer stripped himself naked. This was a routine after every sexual encounter. He would head back to his duplex and take a long shower. It was his redemption for the living paradox he had become in the last five years. As he stood under the shower and turned the knob on, tiny blue lights lit up the cubicle and water cascaded down his broad shoulders. This too was her idea. They were supposed to shower together under these very lights whenever they fought. It was her way of calling truce. Now there were neither any fights, nor any calls for truce. Not in this lifetime at least, he thought with a sinking feeling in his stomach.

Standing still, with his head bowed down, Saveer could feel his thighs ache because of the hundred extra squats he had done earlier that day. He had worked hard for the pain and the more intense it was, the more easily he could divert his mind. Sex too was a pain initiator. Every time he fucked the brains out of a girl, helped her climb unprecedented sexual highs, he felt like spitting on himself. It was a self-inflicted punishment, of telling himself that he had deserved what had happened to him all these years. Saveer knew that if he did not inject pain into himself, he would just be like the living dead. And hadn't she made him promise that he wouldn't waste himself if she died? *Did she always know that she would die?* And even she didn't, he did.

But what was her fault? he wondered. *I tried to keep it a secret from her but it didn't work. I should have told her. At least I could have saved her.* He curled his hand into a fist and hit the coffee-coloured tile in front of him hard. *Her only fault was that she had loved him with all her heart. And what did he do? He killed her.*

4

Forever. Is. A. Lie.

These words didn't let Prisha sleep. They reverberated one at a time as if a mallet was hitting the gong of her conscience. The echo was so loud it shattered the glasses of delusions she had built around her about her relationship with Utkarsh.

She understood that she had had a bloated, false image of Utkarsh in her head. She had looked up at him as a larger-than-life figure, flawless, worshipful. Even though there was a tiny voice in Prisha's head that sought to make her realize that he was not perfect, that their relationship had its shortcomings, she had chosen to ignore it. And that is a cardinal sin we all commit in our relationships. We choose to fall in love with our interpretation of a person and not the person himself. We drown out all voices that contradict our interpretation. As a result, when the relationship ends and we see the person the way he is, in startling clarity, we are shocked and left with nothing but remorse.

'What the fuck are you doing here so early? Didn't you sleep last night?' It was Zinnia. She came out of her bedroom, stifling a yawn. Her hair was dishevelled and she was wearing a pair of skimpy shorts, barely covering her bottom, and a spaghetti top.

'I did, but woke up early,' Prisha lied. She didn't want to share much. Zinnia often took advantage of her two-year seniority to patronize Prisha. At times it worked, but mostly it didn't.

'Did you guys do it?' Zinnia asked, ambling towards the kitchen. She switched on the electric kettle after filling it up with some water from the tap.

'No.' It sounded as if Prisha thought before answering out loud.

'No?' Zinnia sounded surprised. She poured the hot water into a mug. She took out a green tea bag from a box kept on top of the refrigerator. Dipping the tea bag in the hot water, she came back to the living room.

'Why not?' she asked and went to stand outside in the adjacent balcony. Prisha followed her and noticed that her face was flushed. There was also a purple patch of a love bite on her thigh.

'I don't know. Maybe he wasn't in the mood,' Prisha finally responded. One look at her and Zinnia knew the truth.

'I get it. It's okay. I wouldn't have suggested it if I knew you weren't ready.'

'Not your problem. I thought I was,' she said and completed the rest of the sentence in her mind, *ready to destroy myself.* 'What about you?'

'Can't you make that out from my voice?' Zinnia asked. Prisha realized that her voice was slightly hoarse. She knew her question had been rhetorical.

'He was not only what I was told he would be but much more. I tried edging with him for the first time.'

'Edging?'

Zinnia became excited. At first, she seemed to be at a loss for words. Then she composed herself and said, 'Okay, just imagine yourself sitting alone on the world's highest roller coaster. And then you are taken to the peak. You think you will drop down but are pulled back. That feeling of reaching the peak but not tipping over . . . do you get it?'

After a thoughtful pause, Prisha answered, 'No.'

Zinnia looked upset.

'It's prolonging the orgasm, sweets.'

At eighteen, Prisha had only heard of orgasms but had never really experienced one. She had enjoyed having sex for the first time with Utkarsh on her seventeenth birthday. And although she told him, and later her close friends, that she had an orgasm, she was doubtful. Now listening to Zinnia, she was sure it wasn't one.

'What's his name?' Prisha asked. She wanted to shift her focus from anything that could possibly stir up Utkarsh's memories.

'Huh?' For a moment, Zinnia didn't get it and then she said, 'Mean Monster, told you.'

'That can't possibly be a name.'

'I know. But I don't know. Don't think my friend who led me to him knows either.'

'That's weird, isn't it?'

'Yeah, but who cares?' Zinnia finished her green tea and turned around to go back inside.

'I talked to him,' Prisha said. Zinnia stopped in her tracks.

'Talk? He didn't come across as much of a talker.'

'Just a few words.'

'What did he tell you?'

'I was crying so . . .'

Zinnia looked at her flatmate sympathetically. She cupped Prisha's face in her hands and said, 'How many times have I told you to forget Utkarsh? Don't you get it? He never loved you. And there's no reason you should sulk because of that. These things happen. Life doesn't stop. Utkarsh is gone; forget him. Okay?'

Prisha looked at Zinnia. *Easier said than done*, she thought, and nodded.

'Great. So, what did he tell you?'

The four words the Mean Monster had told her echoed within her but she said aloud, 'To take care.'

'Just that?' Zinnia's curiosity dimmed a little by the response.

'Anyway,' she continued, 'Get ready. I have a class. We'll go to college together.' With that, she went inside.

Utkarsh is gone, Prisha replayed Zinnia's words. People leave but the ghost of a dead relationship hovers over the one who loved genuinely. It keeps coming back to haunt every time one thinks one has conquered oneself emotionally. She turned to look up at the clear morning sky and realized that it would be a daunting task to get rid of this ghost.

The good part about studying in a college in a faraway city, away from the friends she grew up with, was that the new ones saw her as she was at present. Prisha wasn't introverted. She could make friends easily and open up without much prodding. She was the one whom friends turned to during a crisis. She was the decision-maker; the most sorted one in her friends circle. But that was when she was in Faridabad. Unfortunately, fate plays its crudest joke on the ones who think they are the most sorted.

It was close to a month in Bengaluru, but Prisha was yet to befriend anyone in her college. There was this one boy though who kept pursuing her. She could see it in his eyes that he was interested in her. But didn't he see what was there in hers?

'You like to eat alone?' It was the same boy: Digambar Sethia. Students called him Diggy. The first thing Prisha had noticed about Diggy were his unnaturally light eyebrows. 'No, nothing like that,' she said. They were in the college canteen, done with the first few lectures.

'Thank god you talk, else my friends had a bet that you could be dumb.' Digambar tried to be funny. It didn't work on Prisha.

'How does it matter? Whether I can talk or not?' she asked with a straight face. Digambar had no answer to that. He took a bite of the burger that he was holding. There was silence. He will leave me alone now, thought Prisha. But he didn't.

'Actually, my friend and I are looking for a third partner,' he said. Prisha noticed that he had a mildly effeminate way of talking.

The obvious question would have been for what, but Prisha surprised him by saying, 'I'm not interested.'

'But you don't know what it is. It is something . . .'

'I don't want to know,' Prisha said, finishing her coffee and standing up. She stashed the paper cup in a bin and turned to see Digambar standing close to her.

'Listen to me once. Please.'

Listen to me, please. Those were her last words to Utkarsh before he had disconnected her call. And she could never contact him again. She was told that she wasn't important enough. Prisha felt an abrupt rage brewing inside her. The next instant she found herself slapping Digambar. It was completely unlike her. But she had become increasingly unpredictable post her break-up.

The slap was so sudden that Digambar didn't know how to react. He was wearing a cap that fell on the ground. Prisha noticed that he was bald. Before he could say anything, Prisha said: 'I know what you have in mind. When I said I'm not interested I thought you would understand. But then let me tell you straight. I'm not interested in you! Just look at you. You think you will be able to impress me by just following me around in college?' And with that, she walked off. Digambar slowly picked up his cap with teary eyes. Looking around, he realized everyone was staring at him with what he was scared of the most: pity.

Once in the classroom, Prisha sat on the last bench and plugged in her earphones. She hid them within her hair. The professor went on lecturing about mass media while she got lost in her own world. Her phone buzzed; it was a message on her cousins' group on WhatsApp. A joke forwarded by Shelly. She looked at the message and then tapped on her number. On an impulse, she checked her profile picture. It was Utkarsh and Shelly. Prisha even knew where the photo had been clicked, in the food court at Ambience Mall, Gurugram. It was the same place that Utkarsh and she had been to innumerable times for *true love* dates.

'What do you think of yourself?' A girl came and nudged her rather aggressively. Prisha pulled out her earphones, taken aback. A quick glance told her that the professor wasn't in the class anymore. Most of the students had dispersed.

'What do you mean?' Prisha asked, standing up.

'How dare you slap my friend?' the girl said. She looked as if Prisha had hit her instead.

'Your friend?' Prisha knew who she was talking about but still feigned ignorance.

'Diggy! How dare you slap him?'

'He was trying to come on to me. I warned him. He had it coming.'

'Oh hello, he wasn't trying to come on to you. He won't ever. We were planning to organize a small group for all our weekend getaway trips and he wanted to know if you were interested.'

'Oh!' Prisha felt a guilt-knot within her.

'And you should have known what he is suffering from before taking a smart-ass jibe at him of whether he deserves you or not.'

'What is he suffering from?' Prisha asked in a small voice.

'Alopecia. If you really aren't a BC then do me a favour, apologize to him. I can't see my best friend crying.' And then the girl walked off.

Prisha immediately googled Alopecia. Alopecia Areata was the loss of body and scalp hair. The light eyebrows, the baldness—it made sense now. But her own impulsive rudeness didn't. She had done to Diggy exactly what Utkarsh had done to her—she had refused to listen to him.

It took half an hour for Prisha to locate the girl who had confronted her, and Digambar. They were sitting

22

in one corner of a rather-empty college library. Prisha walked up to them with a pounding heart. She went and stood before them, guilty. The girl looked up at her.

'You want to say something?'

Prisha nodded. 'I'm sorry Digambar. I didn't know . . .'

There was silence. Digambar looked up at her. His eyes were swollen.

'Are you sorry for my suffering?' he asked. Prisha glanced at the girl next to him and then at Digambar.

'No! I'm sorry for my stupid behaviour,' she said. 'I really didn't mean to hit you. It was just . . .' she paused, and then added, 'I'm sorry.'

Digambar stood up and hugged her. She wasn't ready for such a sudden, intimate response, but she didn't break the embrace.

'Its okay, Prisha. I knew you aren't a bitch deep down. You can call me Diggy,' he said, breaking away from the hug and smiling through his tears. 'Friends?'

Prisha nodded slowly. 'Friends.'

'I'm Gauri,' the girl sitting beside Diggy stood up as well. Prisha extended her hand for a shake.

'We are bros. We hug, we don't shake hands,' Gauri said and gave Prisha a tight hug. She suddenly felt at peace. This is what she needed—friends.

'What was it you said? Weekend getaway?' Prisha inquired.

'So,' Diggy wiped his tears, 'Gauri and I needed another person as we are planning to explore places around Bengaluru from time to time. Three is a crowd and we need a crowd to fund the trips.' Diggy smiled.

'I'm in,' Prisha said.

'Awesome. Day after tomorrow we are going to Nandi Hills, 4.30 a.m.'

It already sounded refreshing to Prisha.

* * *

Nandi Hills looked surreal. It calmed her down and offered her the much-needed soul therapy that she had required all this while. Prisha kept to herself and sat on a rock, soaking in the vastness of nature. The clouds hung low and she wished she could dissolve in them. Diggy and Gauri were busy clicking photos.

'Will you just sit there the whole time? Come here. Let's click a selfie at least?' Diggy interrupted her thoughts.

Prisha wanted to be alone but didn't want to make it obvious. She joined them for a selfie, after which she kept walking along the cliff. She came across a bike—a Harley Davidson. There were two steaming cups of coffee on the pillion seat but nobody around. She walked towards the edge of the cliff. As she cautiously peeped into the abyss, it seemed to call out to her. She felt an urge to jump. There was too much chaos inside her. But was killing herself a solution to ending that chaos? She took a step back and decided to join her friends, which is when she heard the ringtone of a phone kept on the parked bike.

I love you Prisha . . . I love you too . . . I love you Prisha . . . I love you too . . .

It was a man and a woman's voice, one after the other. She frowned. She had distinctly heard her name. She went closer to the bike and looked down at the phone, contemplating whether to pick it up. She was about to touch it when a heavy voice spoke from behind, 'That's my phone.' She turned around to see a man in short hair, wearing a pair of black aviators, a black leather jacket, navy blue denims and trekking shoes. He looked like a professional biker.

'I'm sorry,' she said, not knowing what else to say. Diggy called her from behind.

'Prisha, let's go *yaar.*'

With a few furtive glances at the man, a frowning Prisha headed back towards the car. As she climbed in, she saw the man plug in his earphones. He put the cell phone in his jeans, picked up the two cups of coffee in his hands and went and sat at edge of the cliff. He clinked the two cups and sipped from one. He placed the other cup close to him and kept glancing at it, as if he could see someone in the rising steam of the coffee.

That's my phone. Prisha had heard this voice before. In fact, quite recently. And then it struck her. It was a brief meeting a few nights ago. She asked Diggy to park the car for a minute.

5

She was a like a book to him. The kind you know has been written for you the moment you spot it. It seems so special that at first you get lost in its cover, knowing fully well that the real magic lies inside. Then you start reading it and you feel that you can relate to every word, every emotion. You finish the book, but realize that the story can never end in you. You swear you haven't read such a book before, and you never will. You keep the book in a special corner of your bookshelf, reading and rereading it on a daily basis, discovering things you missed during the first read, making new interpretations. And then one day you can't find the book on the shelf. It has disappeared. But where? You don't know. All that you are left with is a question: did you really read the book or was it just a dream?

Saveer didn't know what was more painful, that there wasn't any such book, or that it didn't belong to him anymore.

Sitting with two cups of coffee, he realized how some people enter your life and change it completely. They act like a mirror to your soul. But when they leave . . . Saveer took a sip of his coffee.

On weekends, he would take her to Lonavla on his bike. They would sit on the cliffs, sipping coffee and watching the sunrise. Everything in life made sense in those moments when she held his arm and put her head on his shoulder. At times, lost in the fragrance of her hair, he would get the urge to tell her everything. *The truth*. But it felt so good to be true with her that he would stop himself from telling her anything, hoping that what she didn't know, wouldn't affect her.

Now, sitting all alone on a cliff at Nandi Hills, Saveer knew that hiding the truth from her was a mistake for which he was paying heavily. He should have alerted her the first time he had fallen for her. That he wasn't capable of certain things in his life, like loving someone. Was he selfish to have not informed her? But doesn't love make one selfish?

Since her death, there had been two Saveers. One, which wanted to escape the fact that such a crisis had ever happened, and another which had built a home around that crisis. The former led him to sexual escapades on weekends while the latter pushed him to visit places alone, where he could feel her presence. The first was terrified of the pain that her death had brought along, but for the second, the same pain was his home.

To mourn the loss of a loved one and to immerse yourself in such suffering is also a part of love that we can't sever ourselves from, no matter how hurtful it is.

Having finished his coffee, he was about to get up when he noticed a shadow behind him. Saveer turned around.

'Are you the Mean Monster?' Prisha asked.

Saveer removed his aviators and stared at her. She looked like a schoolgirl.

6

Saveer wore his aviators and stood up. He was a good five inches taller than she was. His gait was threatening. It made her feel like she shouldn't have come back. It was quiet except for the honking of a few vehicles that were passing by. Prisha noticed him eyeing the Innova behind her.

'State your business,' he said, looking at her.

Does that mean he is the Mean Monster? Prisha wondered and said, 'We've met on a night before, remember?' She presumed he was the one.

'I've selective amnesia.' Not a single muscle on his face twitched.

Prisha tried to decode his look. *Was he serious? Or was he being sarcastic?*

'I'm sorry to disturb you,' she said finally. He was being sarcastic.

'Sorry doesn't change anything. Think before you act,' he said. The rudeness in his voice pricked Prisha.

'Excuse me, it was you who were looking at me the other night. I don't know why you're refusing to recognize me today. But I'm sure it was you who were with my friend.'

'So what if I was? I'm not interested in kids,' he said curtly.

That was unnecessary, Prisha thought, livid inside.

'I'm not here because I'm interested in you. I am interested in what you told me that night.'

Saveer was quiet. His eyes, though, were unfalteringly on her. Prisha was about to speak up when Saveer smirked.

'What are you smirking at?' Prisha asked.

'Your generation will only know that love which doesn't make sense. For the sensible one, you need to dive deep. Deeper than the depth you can imagine.'

Such a presumptuous douche. It was a mistake to approach him.

'I loved the guy, all right? Please don't try to patronize me. It may be in vogue for your generation but I'm just saying . . .'

Saveer cut her short with a piercing look, 'There is a synonym of the kind of love you felt for that guy. I hope you know it.'

Prisha found herself looking expectantly at him.

'It's spelt as J.O.K.E,' he almost sniggered.

Prisha had had enough. She turned to walk back to the car, fuming inside. She may have lost in love but that doesn't mean it wasn't love! Utkarsh was and will be her first love. Period. It had been a beautiful experience with an ugly ending. And she will miss it. But nobody can say it was a . . . what did that douche say? Joke. *Joke? Really?*

As she got inside the car and closed the door loudly, Gauri leaned forward from the back seat and asked, 'Who was that?'

'Hotness,' Diggy said, displaying his phone. He had clicked a zoomed-in picture of Saveer. Prisha snatched the phone from him.

'Seriously?' She glared at Diggy and deleted the picture.

'Come on, he is hot! Why did you delete it?'

Prisha gave him another look and said, 'Can you please drive?'

Diggy stepped on the accelerator. The very next moment someone started honking behind them. He glanced in the rear-view mirror and realized it was Saveer. Diggy was about to move when Prisha said, 'Don't, Diggy. Just don't. Some people don't deserve kindness.' She didn't know who she was referring to in the last part, the man or Utkarsh.

Diggy was confused. The incessant honking irked him.

'Okay, I can't take this anymore,' he said and steered the car to the left. The bike zoomed past them.

'Bastard!' Prisha swore. Diggy and Gauri exchanged glances.

'How many more bastards do you talk to just like that?' Gauri asked.

'Bunk it,' Prisha was in no mood to talk. Gauri shrugged and plugged in her earphones to be with

Coldplay while Diggy remained focused on the road. They had hired the car from a friend's friend, paying only for the fuel.

Prisha rolled down the window and leaned against it after reclining her seat a little. She closed her eyes and as the wind hit her face, she consciously tried to think nothing. Unfortunately, the painful memories of her break-up resurfaced to haunt her. Determined not to succumb to them again, she forced her mind to make a detour. *A man who is outright rude, judgemental and pretty much full of himself, who fucks women as a hobby, looks down on someone's love . . . that kind of a man has a romantic caller tune in his own voice? And that too with her name? Isn't it odd?* The last thought made her sit up. She glanced at Diggy and Gauri guiltily as if she had been caught red-handed. But doing what? She didn't know. Not yet.

7

'**O**f course I talk to you, Mumma,' Prisha said on the phone.

Ever since WhatsApp had introduced video calling, her mother preferred having video chats over voice calls irrespective of whether she was in a Wi-Fi zone or not. And video calls were tricky. You can fake the 'all's well' on voice calls, but to pretend to look like everything was fine each time your mother called could get a little taxing. Some of her cousins knew about Shelly and Utkarsh and so did her parents. Since Prisha had initially pretended that she wasn't wallowing after her break up, she had to put up that pretence all the time, especially during video calls.

'You used to talk more,' her mother complained, trying to adjust the phone camera.

'I have come here to study, Mumma, not for a holiday. I've loads of assignments.'

'I know. Your father told me that. You are having your food on time, right?'

'Yes, Mumma.'

'And your periods? Did it pain as much as it did last month?'

'No, this time it was okay.'

'Good. It means the homeopathic medicine worked. Take it regularly for two more months and the pain will go and the flow will be better.'

'Yes, Mumma, I will.'

'Still no friends?'

'I have made two friends, Gauri and Diggy.'

'I'm so happy to know that. What about . . .'

The inquiries continued and Prisha kept responding. Her father talked to her next, but he had fewer questions. Prisha loved her parents. They had raised her to be fearless but had not mentioned that even the bravest of hearts falters when it tries to take over the fortress of love. Prisha didn't want to cry and tell them that they had failed in their upbringing. She was strong, and this was a temporary phase. After her father, it was her little sister, Ayushee's turn. She took the phone and went to her room. Prisha could see her lock the door and then look at the camera with a shy smile.

'What's up, Mickey?' Prisha asked.

'Di, there is a guy in my coaching class. He keeps looking at me. And I find . . .'

'Stay away from him, Mickey,' Prisha blurted out in a strict voice.

'But Di . . .'

'I don't want to hear anything about it. If he looks at you again, complain about it to your teacher.'

Ayushee was just thirteen. The same age as Prisha when she had first met Utkarsh, also at her coaching class. How she wished she had avoided him then. She noticed Ayushee was a little upset but she said, 'Okay, as you say, Di.'

It was better to be strict now than to see her being sorry about it later. Just then, Prisha's phone buzzed. Diggy was calling. She took his call.

'Yeah Diggy?'

'Gauri has shut the door.'

'Shut the door? What do you mean? Which door?'

'Her bedroom door. She isn't opening the door or answering her phone. I'm scared. Could you please come over fast?'

'Yeah, okay. I'm coming.' Prisha disconnected the phone and, with no clue of the situation whatsoever, booked a cab. She was dressed by the time it arrived. It was a ten-minute drive to Gauri's place. She lived with Diggy in a spacious, well-furnished, 2BHK flat. They had offered Prisha to shift in with them but she wanted some more time to consider it. As of now, she was comfortable with the space Zinnia gave her. With Gauri and Diggy, privacy could be a concern since they were in the same batch.

Diggy opened the door but before he could explain anything, Prisha went straight to Gauri's bedroom. She knocked a few times, asking her to open the door. Diggy joined her.

'She won't open the door. I have been trying since . . .'

Diggy stopped as Gauri opened the door. She pulled Prisha inside and locked the door.

'What's this? Let me in as well!' Diggy screamed.

'Give us five minutes, BC!' Gauri said.

'Okay, I'm waiting here,' Diggy said and placed his ear on the door.

'What happened?' Prisha asked, watching Gauri sit down on the bed.

'I missed my periods.'

Prisha rolled her eyes and sighed. 'Thank God! I kind of guessed it.'

'That I missed my periods?'

'No! That it could be related to your periods.'

'Okay. I had sex last month.'

'You did?' Prisha was genuinely shocked. There are some people who always come across as asexual. Gauri was one such person. At least to Prisha. She noticed Gauri nodding but didn't know whether to ask her who the boy was since they were still in the February of their friendship.

'With Sanjeev,' Gauri said looking down at the floor. Prisha didn't know who he was.

'Sanjeev sir, I mean,' Gauri murmured. Sanjeev Hande was their professor of media studies in college—a forty-five-year-old married man with a son. Prisha couldn't imagine Gauri with him. She wanted to reconfirm.

'That's our media studies professor?'

Gauri nodded.

'What do we do now?' Prisha's voice quivered. She wanted to know more about this dalliance of Gauri's but knew better than to act nosy at this point.

'I was thinking of taking a test but I don't know if I'm ready for it. What if . . .'

Prisha sat down beside her. A minute passed in silence. Two knocks on the door.

'What are you two up to?' Diggy kept asking.

'Shut up, Diggy, please,' Gauri said.

'There's no other option. We have to take the test,' Prisha said. Gauri suddenly held her hand tightly and looked at her. Prisha knew Gauri was looking for confidence. And she couldn't let her down.

'Give me some time,' Prisha said standing up.

'Don't let Diggy know about this. He is a little judgemental. I don't want him to . . .'

'Relax. It will forever be between you and me,' she said and went out of the room. Diggy was hysterical as he rushed inside Gauri's room immediately and confronted her. Meanwhile, Prisha went out and after locating a chemist's shop nearby, bought a pregnancy test kit.

'She is damn sentimental about her family. Now she is all right,' Diggy said as he opened the door for Prisha to come in. She understood Gauri had fed him a false story.

'Actually!' she said and went to Gauri's room. Gauri took the kit and went to the toilet. Standing alone in her room, Prisha felt like her old self once again—back when she was in Faridabad and would always take decisions on behalf of her friends and stand by them. The way Gauri had looked at her when she was holding her hand was a reminder of who she had been before Utkarsh had broken her. Prisha was happy and grateful to have met Gauri and Diggy at this point in her life. Her thoughts were interrupted as Gauri came out. She dashed towards Prisha and held her in a tight embrace.

'You are my lucky charm, Prisha. My eggs were too snobbish for the sperms.'

Prisha smiled slightly. 'Be careful next time,' she said.

Gauri nodded. So there would be a next time, which meant it wasn't a one-time affair. Most probably, they had had a history. *But he is way older than she is*, Prisha thought. The two girls suddenly felt a bear hug and realized that Diggy had joined them.

'I also want to cry or smile or whatever it is that you two are doing.'

'We are smiling, dumbo!' Prisha said and tightened the hug.

'Let's drink tonight? I'm tired of the college assignment shit,' Diggy proposed.

'I so need a drink,' Gauri said and winked at Prisha, leaving Diggy to keep looking from one to the other without any clue.

* * *

The three went to No Limmits. Gauri ordered a Long Island Ice Tea, Diggy ordered a beer while Prisha ordered white rum with red bull. The music was loud. It was Bollywood night. The lights were psychedelic and the dance floor was inviting. Prisha excused herself to go to the washroom.

While Prisha was washing her hands, a woman stepped out of a toilet cubicle, looking rather nervous. She was dolled up and was kept checking herself in the mirror. She didn't look a day older than twenty-five. Soon, the woman's phone rang.

'I thought it was him,' she told someone over the phone. 'No. Not yet. I'm so damn excited and nervous. He told me he would text me when he gets here. Is that the Mean Monster's style? Okay. I don't know. I guess I need a smoke.'

Prisha had almost stopped listening to the girl until she heard the name Mean Monster. One look at her and Prisha knew she was his *prey* like Zinnia was. Prisha got out of the washroom and joined Diggy and Gauri outside. Her eyes, however, remained fixed on the washroom door. Soon, the woman came out and sat at a table, alone.

'What?' Gauri asked, following Prisha's gaze. The girl was now fidgeting with her bag.

'That girl,' Prisha said, 'will go to the smoking zone in a few seconds.'

'So?' Gauri turned to look at Prisha.

'How long can you keep her busy in the smoking room?'

'I can, for some time, but why would I do that?' Gauri said.

Prisha thought for a moment before responding. 'I want to spoil some presumptuous douchebag's night, that's why,' she said and gulped down the rest of her drink.

8

He felt happy on such nights. Not just because he had a sexual release but due to the punishment he inflicted upon himself by reminding himself that he did not deserve anything good. Sex with strangers without any emotions, without owing anything to them, without anything at stake, with pure animal instinct, was the lowest he could stoop down to. It was necessary, although no one would understand that.

We all seek ways to feel good about ourselves, to convince ourselves that we deserve good things. But not Saveer. His purpose of existence since his girlfriend's death was to keep reminding himself that he was a bad person.

Saveer didn't know who had named him the Mean Monster. All he did was keep his real name a secret. But he knew very well why he had been given the moniker, and it stuck. He didn't give a damn. He had read somewhere that souls never die. And so, even though he had witnessed her body burn to ashes in front of his eyes, he felt her soul must still be watching him.

She had been crushed beyond identification in the accident. On the night she was cremated, it wasn't just her body that had charred, so had Saveer's hopes, dreams and promises. Only the worst part of their love story stayed alive: Him.

Saveer was done getting ready. Tonight was no different. He would go to the pub where his blind date was waiting. He would either take her to her place or to a hotel, fuck her, feel filthy about himself and come back home. Sometimes redemption is about how much you can destroy yourself—one night at a time.

It took him forty minutes to reach the pub. His date was waiting for him. Saveer had a separate SIM for his sexual liaisons. He switched it on when he was ready, which was mostly on weekends, and after he was done with the girl, he removed the SIM. 'No calls, only messages.' Initially, he would hook up through a dating app, but in the last three years, he only had to switch on his phone and the proposals poured in in abundance. The Mean Monster had slowly started ruling over the girls' minds, but he was indifferent to it. He just had to choose. Saveer had no preference. He chose randomly and never repeated the girls. Importantly, he never got emotionally involved with anyone.

Saveer entered No Limmits. It took him a trice to spot the table where the girl had said she would be waiting. As he approached the table, the girl turned around casually. And spotted him. But she wasn't who Saveer had expected. He had met this girl before. And he didn't want to meet her again.

9

One look at her and Saveer knew where he had seen her. In the last five years, she was the only girl he had met thrice in quick succession and at various places. She was the only girl who had seen him both as the Mean Monster and as Saveer Rathod, although he wasn't sure if she knew his name.

'Hi, I'm Prisha. You may not know me,' the girl said. Saveer took his time to sit opposite her at the table.

'Hi, I'm Nobody,' Saveer replied sarcastically.

'Nice to meet you, Nobody. But honestly, I was expecting a Who-Are-You?' Prisha said. The thrill in her voice hinted that she had a plan. It wasn't just a coincidence that she was sitting in front of him instead of the woman he was supposed to be with. *But why?* he wondered, looking straight into her eyes.

He has captivating eyes, Prisha thought and realized that the silence between them wasn't helpful. She quickly put together what she would say next. 'So, have you been cured of your selective amnesia?'

After a brief pause, Saveer said, 'I don't fuck kids.'

Prisha's jaw dropped somewhat in surprise.

'Excuse me! I'm eighteen, not a kid. And also, I'm not interested in doing anything with you,' she said, returning his stare. *His eyes were more than captivating, they were hypnotic*, she realized.

'And still you are here, sitting right in front of me, knowing fully well who I am and what my intentions are.' He smirked, adding, 'Or did I rub off some of the selective amnesia on to you?'

She noticed the arresting smirk. She now knew why it had taken him two minutes to get Zinnia out of the pub the other night.

'I'm immune to that. You won't be able to rub off anything on to me,' she said. He started tapping his fingers on the table and smirked again.

'Forget it,' he said and was about to get up when Prisha held his hand rather impulsively. He looked at her in surprise; she released her grip.

'Giving up so easily is such an old-fashioned thing to do. Oh, I'm sorry you are not really eighteen, are you?' The I-wasn't-ready-for-this look on his face told her she had had her revenge. There was a hint of smile on her lips. She was happy to have had the upper hand this time. That was her only reason to intercept him tonight.

Saveer sat down. He sighed and said, 'When you always have the person you love by your side, you get to know a little about love. When you can't have a person you love, you get to know more about love. But when a person you love is snatched away from you, you wish you had never known love at all. Unless you have experienced such terrible grief, do not ever assume that you have loved someone truly. In fact, there is nothing called true love. However, there is something called complete love. And most of us are arrogant enough to assume our incomplete love as complete. You are no different.

'At the age of eighteen, you have probably been in one relationship so far? Maybe two? And you think you have experienced complete love? No! You told me that you've had a break-up. Trust me, it is nothing compared to losing a loved one, which can be far more defeating than death itself. Such an experience can leave you completely unanchored, unhinged. It can take away your zest for life; there is no essence left, only existence.

'A break-up isn't that debilitating. A break-up still has room for hope. Hope of another chance, another someone. But losing a loved one offers no such awning.' Saveer paused. He realized that he had said more than he had intended to.

'So,' he summed up, 'cry as much as you want to but trust me, you haven't yet experienced complete love. My advice is, save your tears for the day you get to know complete love. But I hope you don't get there.' His gaze remained steadfastly on her.

Prisha licked her lips, realizing they had gone dry. 'You loved this person . . . a lot, isn't it?' The answer was obvious and still she found herself asking him.

His jaws locked. His gaze was still fixed on her. Prisha felt as if someone had put all ambient noise on mute. If eyes could kill, his tore her into a thousand pieces at that moment. Never before had she seen such intense pain in someone's eyes. Not even in her own.

'None of your business,' he said and stood up to leave, when a girl called him from behind.

'Hey!' She sounded nervous. 'Sorry, I got caught up with a stupid person,' she said, coming closer to them.

Prisha knew who the *stupid person* was, but at that moment, she wished Gauri had engaged the girl for some more time. She had wanted to spoil the Mean Monster's night but . . . Saveer put his arm around the girl's waist and whispered, 'Patience is a vice when it comes to a night like this.'

'Precisely what I felt,' the girl said. Her mouth had gone dry. He was exactly like she had been told he would be: confident, hypnotic and someone who didn't waste time. He held her tight and they made their way towards the exit, leaving Prisha behind. Gauri joined her. It took her a couple of shoulder-taps to break Prisha's trance. They went to join Diggy.

Saveer rode the bike at full speed, the girl's arms wrapped around his waist. On other nights, he would have told his date where they were heading, to a hotel or to her place. But tonight he didn't. He rode without a destination, a single question hammering his mind: *You loved her a lot, isn't it?* The speedometer needle swung dangerously towards the maximum speed. The girl tightened her grip on his waist.

'I guessed you'd have a thing for speed,' she yelled over the wind whipping against their faces. She was expecting an acknowledging nod. But he soon slowed down and parked the bike on a dark, deserted road. The girl thought that she had said something wrong. She was about to clarify when he grabbed her butt and kissed her neck. The ferocity of the butt-squeeze made her understand that this was it; the place where the Mean Monster would take her. She felt adventurous, doing it by the side of a road.

She was wearing a little black dress and high heels. Saveer relaxed his grip on her butt and then pinned her hands behind her head. He slipped a hand under her dress. The touch of his cold fingers on her warm thighs gave her goosebumps. She instinctively pressed her legs together. But he forced his way upward till he reached her thong. As he rubbed her vagina, he realized she was already wet. The girl had closed her eyes. It was too good to be true. He pressed his lips on the nape of her neck and held her close. But her eyes flew open when she realized that he had ripped apart her thong. He hung it on the bike's handlebar. Then he put his hand under her dress again and used his middle finger to slowly make its way inside her wet lips while biting her shoulder.

She somehow managed to release herself from his clutch and turned around. He held her breasts and thrust his finger into her vagina. Pleasure made her rub her butt against his groin, feeling his hardness. At that moment, the girl could only think of sex but Saveer had something else on his mind, which he could not set aside even during the sexual act. As the intensity of the question—*You loved her a lot, isn't it?*—kept increasing, so did his fingering. It wasn't really the question that troubled him but the answer. The answer threatened to break open the gates he had held closed for so long. Her face kept coming back to him—when he had seen her for the first time, and when he saw her for the last time . . .

'Oh fuck!' The girl cried out, succumbing to the pleasure.

'I want you to do me. NOW!' she moaned aloud. Saveer pulled out his finger and spread her legs. In no time, he was inside her. The thickness made her lock her jaw while the length made her eyes roll back. The relentless thrusts took away the girl's sense of time. He was her only support on that dark stretch. She gripped his arm that was wound around her breasts tightly. She opened her eyes only when she felt a semi-warm liquid flowing down the sides of her thighs. She was huffing. Not him. She was glad he hadn't come inside her. Saveer dropped her at her place. Not a single word was exchanged between the two. She was expecting a small peck but Saveer was distracted.

Loved every bit of it, Monster, she mumbled, holding on to her torn thong and watching him ride off into the night.

That night neither Prisha nor Saveer knew that they were in each other's thoughts. It was like footprints on a virgin beach, an exploratory mission to discover the unknown. In matters of the heart, any such discovery could wreak emotional havoc and it was this destruction that brought one face-to-face with one's naked self. However, Saveer, still reeling from his past experiences, had made a rule: Nobody should occupy his heart again. Except the ones he had killed.

Sitting with Gauri and Diggy in the pub, Prisha realized that she wasn't thinking about Utkarsh after a long time. There was something else to think about . . . her heart quickly corrected the statement, or was it *someone*?

10

It was when the Mean Monster had walked away with the girl that Prisha realized that she had been unknowingly looking for what he had just given her: a different perspective. She just didn't have the courage to convince herself that she could harbour different feelings for Utkarsh. That's why humans can't live in isolation. We need others to take us to those points within ourselves that we avoid.

While she remained lost in thoughts, Gauri was curious to know why she had been asked to keep the girl occupied. 'What was the need?' she asked. Prisha didn't answer. She was already in conflict. *What if it wasn't love that she had felt for Utkarsh?* Just because he had been the first boy in her life, her first relationship and the first time she had experienced those feelings, didn't necessarily mean that it had to be love. We all have our make-believe prisons, created by our interpretations of our relationships. A part of us wants to break free and a part wants to stay imprisoned. It's a dilemma most people go through. Until the Mean Monster had explained what complete love was, Prisha hadn't felt the urge to break free from her self-made prison.

She suddenly felt relieved. A seed of hope had been planted in her heart and she saw a glimpse of the road ahead. Possibilities are for a love-struck heart what spring is for a bud.

After several rounds of drinks, the three friends made their way to Gauri and Diggy's flat. They were in a cab and Prisha stayed quiet. Her head was reeling after all the rum she had had. Plus the alcohol revealed a subtext to everything. The way she impulsively held his hand, the way he looked at her when he first saw her. She kept shaking her head to ward off his thoughts but they continued to come back to her. Gauri, sitting beside Prisha in the back seat of the cab, suddenly started sobbing. Diggy turned back and exchanged a look with Prisha. Neither said anything till Prisha asked the driver to stop next to a small, unkempt garden in front of their apartment. They helped Gauri out of the cab and stepped into the garden. There was a nip in the air. The three settled down on a bench. 'I'm sorry guys,' Gauri broke the silence. 'What happened?' Prisha asked, but Gauri didn't answer. Prisha held her face and asked again.

'Won't you tell us?'

Gauri started sobbing. 'It was supposed to be casual but I fell for him.'

Both Diggy and Prisha knew who she was talking about. It was their professor.

'He had clearly told me that he is way older to me, he has a family and it will all be casual but . . .' Gauri couldn't finish her sentence and hugged Prisha.

When you love someone but can't have that person, you get to know more about love. The Mean Monster's words came back to her as she comforted Gauri.

'Shit happens,' Prisha said. She was finding it difficult to switch roles. Her own emotional injuries needed nursing but she had to play the nurse to Gauri now.

'But I don't want to be the other woman in his life. That's the only thing I've hated and that's what I have become,' Gauri said. 'I am going to the flat,' she said, breaking away from the embrace and hurried off. Prisha wanted to follow but Diggy stopped her.

'She needs to be alone,' he said. Prisha understood and decided to sit with him.

'I had told her to be careful. I didn't like that scoundrel from day one. If he has a wife and a family then what the fuck is he doing having an affair with someone half his age?' Diggy sounded bitter.

Prisha responded a moment later, 'Maybe it's not love.'

'I told her that. He doesn't love her.'

'No, I mean for Gauri.'

'If it isn't, then why is she upset?'

'Maybe she thinks it is love.'

Diggy kept looking at Prisha for some added explanation but her eyes were fixed on the night sky.

'Why would you say that? She seemed pretty genuine in her love to me,' he finally asked again.

'Even I was sure it was genuine,' she said, not referring to Gauri.

'Then why are you saying so? Are you drunk?' Diggy held her hand instinctively. He was not sure if she was okay. Prisha nodded and said, 'Let's go be with her. We don't have to say anything. Maybe she only wanted us to listen and not give her a pep talk.' She stood up, Diggy followed.

As they entered the lane to their apartment, the sight ahead made them freeze in their tracks. Three men were trying to molest Gauri. She couldn't yell for help as one of the men had clamped his hand over her mouth. Both Prisha and Diggy charged at the men, screaming at the tops of their lungs. One of them kicked Diggy in the stomach and he fell on the ground. The other man held Prisha from behind. She tried to bite him to free herself, but he punched her so hard that she blacked out instantly. The men dashed to their car, which was parked nearby, even as Gauri was screaming hysterically.

* * *

Prisha didn't know what time it was when she opened her eyes. She could hear someone saying something to her. The words made no sense. When she could somewhat focus her eyes on the person who was talking to her, she was convinced that she was in a dream. Why else would the Mean Monster appear in front of her out of nowhere? She slipped back into unconsciousness.

11

When Prisha opened her eyes again, she realized she was in a hospital. She slowly lifted her head. On her right, lay Gauri and on her left, Diggy. Prisha remembered seeing Diggy collapse in the lane after being kicked by one of the men. They had witnessed Gauri being . . . and she remembered everything. *Was Gauri all right?* She turned to see her smiling at her.

'You were punched. Diggy was kicked. I was punched and kicked and groped,' Gauri sounded like the experience had been an achievement for her.

'Thanks for the news,' Prisha said sarcastically. 'How are you?'

'My thigh still hurts. That's where the BCs had kicked me. But no fracture. Rest is fine. And you?'

Prisha tried to move, only to realize that her body felt stiff and her jaws hurt the most.

'Just my jaws. Rest is fine.'

'Our phones are with them. I asked the nurse. By the way, I heard her say that they'll release us today.'

'How long has it been?' Prisha suddenly realized that while she had told Zinnia that she'd be staying back with Gauri and Diggy last night, she had not informed her mother.

'It's just the next morning. It's been ten hours since we were admitted to the hospital.'

Prisha relaxed. She could call her mother and tell her that she had woken up late since it was a Sunday. She knew her parents. If they caught so much as a whiff of what had happened they would make sure she moved to the college hostel and stayed there till her graduation. It would have been okay with her had she not met Gauri and Diggy. But not anymore.

'Please tell me we are alive.' It was Diggy. He sounded weak.

'Come on, you were only kicked once, not stabbed,' Gauri said.

'It felt the same,' he groaned.

'Who brought us here?' he asked. It was an interesting question. Gauri was molested. They were attacked. Then who got them here? A Good Samaritan?

'Some man brought us here.'

Some man? Really? Prisha thought and immediately remembered seeing the Mean Monster. *Wasn't that a dream?* She wondered.

'Why would a random guy admit us in a hospital?' Diggy said.

Of course, he recognized me! Prisha was confident. His face flashed before her eyes as his words buzzed in her ears. There was an attractive genuineness in the way he spoke to her. Although she didn't know him, she felt as if she could rely on him. Prisha felt an irresistible urge to know him more. His words were like those hauntingly silent nights that prompt an urge to introspect. And by Jove, did he guide her!

There has to be a name, she thought. There had to be a man behind the monster. The latter had to be a facade. Her gut told her that someone who spoke about complete love couldn't just be a sex maniac going around the city fucking women. He had to be someone who was as injured as her, if not more. It was evident in the way he talked about love. Injury and wisdom were soulmates, she now knew. She remembered reading somewhere that when two souls bond over injuries, they heal each other beyond any possible tangible repair. She would have to find him in order to repair herself. Not necessarily to bond with him but because she knew he had the answers to her questions. And if he really admitted them in the hospital because of her then this would be interesting, Prisha told herself.

The doctor came and checked them one at a time. He asked them to take rest for a few days and told the nurse to prepare their release forms. An inspector and a constable came in next and recorded Gauri's statement. They informed her that the lane had been under surveillance for the past few weeks after the police had received similar complaints.

Two hours later, the three friends were in the lobby of the hospital. They were pleasantly surprised when they were informed that their bill had been paid.

'I wish he also took care of our daily booze,' Diggy joked and booked an Uber. Gauri got busy updating her social media about the incident while Prisha went and inquired at the hospital reception about the identity of the person who had hospitalized them. It was important for her to know his name. Other women may know him as the Mean Monster but she was sure he hadn't told them about his concept of complete love. The receptionist checked the records on her computer and said, 'G-Punch—an NGO.'

G-Punch? Prisha quickly googled it. The search results threw up a website. G-Punch was Girl Punch—a complaint cell that addressed harassment against women, working in collaboration with Bangalore Police. It was registered as a non-profit organization. There was a twenty-four-hour toll-free helpline number as well. Prisha scrolled down to see a section which stated that if anyone wanted to register their locality for CCTV coverage in order to safeguard against possible attacks on women, they could fill up a form. She scrolled up and clicked on the *about us* section. There was a profile.

She skipped reading it as her eyes spotted a thumbnail at the bottom of the screen. The name underneath the picture read: Saveer Rathod.

He was the Mean Monster. Prisha smiled even though her jaws still hurt.

12

'You were in a hospital? And I'm supposed to know about it now that you are out?' Zinnia sounded angry and rightfully so. She was the unofficial guardian of Prisha in the city, appointed so by her parents. As planned, Prisha told her mother that she had woken up late since she was up standing at might. Her mother bought the story, advised her a little about her health and that was it. But it was Zinnia's reaction that she was not prepared for.

'I'm sorry. I was unconscious else I would have,' Prisha made a puppy face. Zinnia was preparing a turmeric face pack for herself. She went and hugged her from behind.

'Okay. Don't do it again. No place is safe. Even if you have to move out, stay with a group,' Zinnia said.

'Okay, Ma'am,' Prisha said, breaking her embrace.

'Shut up.'

'Listen, Zin,' Prisha said, 'I think I know who the Mean Monster is.'

Zinnia stopped and turned around in a flash.

'You're kidding!'

'Saveer Rathod. That's his real name.'

'Oh my God! Seriously?'

Prisha nodded.

'How do you know?'

'It's a guess but I think I'm right. He runs an NGO called G-Punch. There must have been a CCTV in the lane where we were accosted, which was probably being monitored by the NGO volunteers. When they saw what was happening, they rushed to rescue us. He was there too. They admitted us to the hospital.'

'But you haven't seen him? How do you . . . ?'

'I have seen him. I told you when he was here we had a little chat.' *And then I met him at Nandi Hills and at the pub.* Prisha didn't tell her about the other two times. Zinnia washed her hands and got busy with her phone.

'I have searched him on Facebook, Twitter, Instagram, Tumblr, Snapchat. He is nowhere,' Prisha said.

'Is he on Tinder?'

'I've no idea, but I guess he isn't.'

Zinnia looked confused, then sighed. 'You are probably right. He isn't. Gosh! I can't forget that night.' Her face flushed and then she got back to her turmeric mixture. Prisha didn't know why her words made her uncomfortable. The kind of discomfort one feels when someone else is enjoying one's precious possession.

'Do tell me if you get to know more about him,' Zinnia said.

'Sure,' Prisha promised and swore to herself that she wouldn't share another word about Saveer with her. She excused herself and went to take a shower.

Turning the shower knob on, Prisha slowly sank to the floor. Water drenched the upper half of her body while the other half remained dry. Just like Utkarsh, through his action, had left her one half dry and now Saveer, with his words, had drenched the other half. She could only think of him since he had left the pub the previous night. She felt as if her present were eclipsing her past, resulting not in darkness, but an unlikely light. Was it for the best? Was she already obsessing over another man? Tears welled up in her eyes. How stubbornly had she concluded that whatever she had felt for Utkarsh was love. And all it took was another man and a few words from him to question it all. Is forever really a lie? And what about *complete love*? Will she ever experience it? She could feel a desperation building up inside her. The same kind that pushes one towards a self-destructive decision. The same kind that makes you believe that perhaps you have fallen in love. At that moment, she only wanted one thing: to meet Saveer again. Only he could help her in this war of emotions raging inside her.

There was a knock on the door. 'Your friends are here,' Prisha heard Zinnia say. She took a deep breath, stood up and wiped her tears.

The three friends had decided to bunk classes that day. After Zinnia left for college, they sat in the living room, watching television on mute.

'I can't believe we are alive,' Diggy said.

'Don't be dramatic. Please,' Gauri said scornfully. Diggy made a face at her.

'Thanks to the NGO,' Prisha said.

'True that,' Gauri seconded.

'I think we should visit the person and thank him. What do you say?' Prisha suggested.

Gauri and Diggy exchanged looks.

'We can,' Gauri said, sensing there was more to it.

'Where do we get the address?' Diggy asked.

'It is on Church Street. The NGO office,' Prisha blurted, a little too quickly.

'We don't even know the name of the NGO and you cared to mug up the address? Are we missing anything?' Gauri asked, looking amused.

'Saveer Rathod,' Prisha said, realizing that Gauri had more or less cracked it anyway.

'*Ahaan*, so finally you open up,' she smiled.

'That's a sexy name. Saveer,' Diggy chipped in.

'How long has it been?' Gauri asked, leaning forward. She was excited to know the details.

'I know him for the last ten days or so. We have met thrice and maybe talked for eight to ten minutes,' Prisha said.

There was silence. 'You can't be serious,' Gauri finally said.

'I stated facts.'

'You are telling us that you are in love with someone you've known for ten days, met thrice and talked perhaps for less than ten minutes?' Diggy was at his melodramatic best.

Prisha looked at him. 'I didn't say love. I'm . . . interested.'

'Ah, okay!' Gauri had disappointment etched all over her face.

'Do you know which college he is in?' Diggy asked.

'No idea.'

'Hence, we should meet this boy who works with the NGO and thank him for helping us. The rest I'm sure Prisha will manage. What say?' Gauri winked at Prisha. She gave a tight smile in response.

'He doesn't work there. He owns it,' Prisha said.

'Oh! Running an NGO at our age! Wow!' Diggy exclaimed. Prisha didn't bother to correct Diggy.

'So should we go?' Gauri asked. The other two gave a thumbs-up.

Prisha copied the address of G-Punch from its website on to her phone's GPS. They reached the office within an hour. It was a bungalow turned into an office. The three had to wait for half an hour before being ushered inside. Gauri and Diggy were both surprised to see a man, and not a boy, sitting in front of them. He was attractive and Diggy had a feeling that he had seen him before but he couldn't remember where.

'We came here to thank you for helping us last night. Thankfully, we didn't sustain any major injuries,' Prisha said, taking the lead. She had prepared the opening line in advance; she didn't want to be tongue-tied like she usually was in front of him. 'You don't thank someone for doing their duty,' Saveer said. He was sitting behind a huge desk, with a Mac and some papers in front of him. He was wearing glasses but had removed them the moment they entered the room. Diggy, Gauri and Prisha were sitting opposite him.

'Still. And I'm also sorry,' Prisha continued.

'Sorry?'

'For being rude the other night.'

Saveer looked at her intently, then said, 'I think we are meeting for the first time.'

'Listen, I said I'm sorry for being rude the other night.' Prisha almost sounded like she was pleading.

'I've no idea what you are talking about. I'm meeting you for the first time.' Saveer sounded confident as if he really hadn't met Prisha before.

'Maybe there has been some misunderstanding,' Gauri chipped in, sensing an awkward silence taking over.

'I'm sure of that. Anyway, I've work. If there's anything else . . .'

'Nothing else,' Prisha said and walked out. She had gone to him nursing hope. And therein lay the problem.

'Thanks again,' Diggy said and followed the girls out. Once outside the bungalow, Gauri asked, 'Are you sure this is the man?'

'Why do I get a feeling like I've seen him before?' Diggy mumbled to himself.

Prisha nodded. 'More than sure. He is the Mean Monster'.

'Mean what?' Diggy frowned. So did Gauri.

'Doesn't matter. You saw him the other day when we went to Nandi Hills.' She clarified to Diggy.

'That hot guy!' Diggy exclaimed.

'But didn't you call him a bastard that day?' Gauri said.

'That's because he was a snob back then who didn't recognize me,' Prisha said, without looking at her.

'And now?' Gauri asked.

'He is still a snob but someone who'll recognize me soon enough.' Prisha said and started walking.

'Why would he recognize you now?' Gauri asked, raising her voice slightly and running to catch up with her.

'Because I'll make sure he does. I won't lose the second time. I can't afford to,' she said, feeling a lump in her throat.

Gauri was clueless. So was Diggy.

13

It was late and the streets were almost empty. Saveer was driving back in his car, trying to find a radio station playing songs that best suited his mood. Since the three teenagers had left his office in the morning, he kept asking himself why he had refused to acknowledge that he was the Mean Monster. Was it because he wanted to be rude to that girl? *No*. Was it because he didn't want her, or anybody else for that matter, to know that Saveer Rathod and the Mean Monster were one and the same person? *No*. Was it because he never wanted anybody to know that Saveer Rathod *could be* the Mean Monster—not even himself? *Yes*. He used to believe in his heart of hearts that he was a one-woman-man but he had now turned into a beast feasting on female flesh. But that's what some of life's wounds turns one into: a living contradiction. His love, had she been alive, would have hated him if she saw what he had turned into. But he had loved her and he had seen the results. He couldn't rely on love anymore.

Saveer had no parents, no siblings and no friends. He only had her: *Ishanvi Rajput*. He had met her during his worst emotional crisis, at the age of twenty-three. He had recently lost his best friend—the only person he was closest to after his parents' death. Saveer had met Ishanvi, Isha for him, on a bus from Pune to Mumbai. He was going back home after attending his best friend's funeral.

Saveer used to work as an investment banker. Everything was still fresh in his mind, as if it had happened just a few minutes ago. She had borrowed his power bank to charge her phone during the journey. He had fallen asleep and when he awoke in Mumbai, Isha wasn't in her seat. An inquiry of the conductor had revealed that Isha had got down at Navi Mumbai. The surprise came three days later in the form of a courier. It was his power bank and a note: *Thanks for leaving an address on the power bank. (BTW, who does that?) I'm ready to believe it wasn't your way of showing an interest in me, if you believe I didn't intend to steal your power bank.* There was a smiley and a phone number as well. The note made him smile after a long time. He had a habit of writing down his address on all his belongings since childhood. He had never imagined that it would lead him to someone as special as her someday.

In the days that followed, Saveer and Isha met and then dated, soon realizing that they were meant for each other. Saveer was an introvert and the fact that Isha pulled him out his comfort zone with her madness was something he couldn't help but admire. It was like god had deprived him of something and Isha had given it back to him. That's how soulmates were created, or so he believed. And now she had left him too. *All because of him*. He should have told her the truth from day one. But then he had been selfish to have her by his side. The truth could have possibly pushed her away. Saveer stepped on the accelerator and reached home in a few minutes.

The house was exactly as he had left it in the morning: in chaos. After freshening up, he took out some frozen chicken from the refrigerator, chopped some veggies and made a chicken-pepper salad. He grabbed a beer from the fridge and sat down at the dining table to have his dinner. He tried to keep his mind blank like he usually did when he was at home—the house Isha and he had planned to share. Suddenly he felt choked and started sobbing. He gulped down the beer to calm himself. It had become a routine and yet he hadn't found a way to stop his tears in the last five years. Their story had aged but the pain continued to stay young. He left the bowl and the can on the table and went to his bedroom.

As he threw himself on the bed, the phone rang. It was from his accounts team. He picked it up.

'Sorry to bother you at this hour, sir,' the accounts employee said.

'What is it?' Saveer sounded neither disturbed nor eager.

'We have a request from the hospital where we had admitted the three kids last night.'

'What's the request?'

'They informed us that the payment for the kids has already been made in cash. So they have requested us to take our cheque back.'

Saveer sat up on the bed. 'Who paid?'

'Isha.'

'What?' Saveer was incredulous.

'I'm sorry, sir. The name is Prisha. Prisha Srivastav. She is one of the girls who were admitted.'

There was silence for a few seconds.

'Cancel the cheque,' Saveer said and hung up. He had seen such high-on-hormones teenagers before. They irritated him. *Whatever they do was to basically seek attention. They have more opinions than knowledge. They see attachment as attraction and then sulk, not able to enjoy either. They claim to be in love when in reality they do not have even an iota of an idea of what love is. One good conversation and they are in love. They overrate commitment but remain confused about loyalty. They underrate sex just to experience it. They are an emotional duality.* Saveer played a Pandit Ravi Shankar piece and lulled himself to sleep.

Next morning he woke up, showered, got dressed and left for office. Little did he notice that the salad bowl that he had left on the dining table the previous night was in the kitchen sink in the morning.

14

Prisha had attended three lectures so far. She was restless and kept fiddling with her phone. She was expecting someone from G-Punch to call her anytime now. The person would inquire why she had initiated the payment and it would give her another chance to meet Saveer. Was it a casual crush, a mere infatuation, a fatal attraction, or something more? Prisha didn't know, nor did she care to label it just yet. All she knew was that he was on her mind day and night. And she had to do something about it. She had to meet him again.

Diggy chose to attend the communications class while the girls took a tea break.

'I never asked you this . . .' Gauri began.

'Asked what?'

'Is this G-Punch man your first? Or have you had other relationships before?' Gauri was dying to know ever since they had left the G-Punch office the other day.

'I was in a relationship. Broke up before coming here.'

'Like a genuine relationship or . . . ?'

'Honestly, when I was in it, I felt it was genuine. At least I was. Then after five years, I understood he was not genuine in his love. And now when I look back at it, I think it was genuine all right, but it wasn't real.' A pause later she added, 'It's confusing, right?'

'Not really. I do get it. Not everything genuine is as real as you want it to be.'

'Actually! Maybe that's because it is purely subjective.'

'Maybe. But what about this G-Punch guy?'

'His name is Saveer.'

'Yeah, Saveer, right.'

'All I know is that I want to know more about him.'

'Hmm.' Gauri thought for a moment and then laughed out loud.

'What?' Prisha looked at her.

'We have both fallen for men who are way older to us. I always knew I was a weirdo. Good to know I'm not the only one.'

Prisha smiled and high-fived her.

'Well, in my case I have been with a boy my age. So, it's something different.'

'Does it give you a kick? An older man? Not an uncle-type, of course, but someone who is . . .'

'Mature, confident, knows life better than me, can be relied upon, is sorted emotionally . . . oh yeah, that's surely a kick,' Prisha completed her line.

'You missed the *sexually experienced* bit,' Gauri winked and they both laughed.

When they were back in class for the last lecture of the day, Prisha kept looking at the list she'd made in her notebook a night ago of the things she knew about Saveer:

1. *His name is Saveer Rathod.*
2. *Goes by the name Mean Monster in the Bangalore party circuit.*
3. *There's no knowing when he meets women but has a different phone number for his escapades.*
4. *Has a ringtone on his phone that says 'I love you, Prisha'. Or did I hear wrong?*
5. *Runs an NGO.*
6. *No social media accounts.*
7. *Not much information on Google either.*

She kept wondering about the fourth point throughout the lecture. Maybe his girlfriend's name was also Prisha—that would be the most obvious answer unless she had heard it wrong. Once the class was over, the three friends decided to go to Forum Mall. Gauri and Diggy kept complaining about the number of assignments they were supposed to do, but Prisha was lost in her own world. 'Oh madam, what? Did you even care to know what the assignments are?' Diggy said, nudging Prisha.

'Nothing will go inside my head until I . . .'

'Until you?' Gauri asked almost immediately.

'Until I meet Saveer again.'

'What's with this sudden obsession?' Diggy looked at her, curious.

'Even I don't know. Why did he not recognize me? I knew he did but he shouldn't have been so cold. It was really very . . .'

'Bad. We know,' Diggy said.

'Sexy!' Prisha rebutted, much to her friends' surprise. 'The more elusive he is, the more I want to demystify him. The more he says he doesn't recognize me, the more I want to stand in front of him. By the way, do you guys think he was he doing it intentionally?' She glanced at the other two for an answer.

'Is he your first?' Diggy asked.

'No. But Utkarsh, my ex, was a joke. I am convinced now. We dated for some years and then he fell for my cousin sister. And if he can fall in love again then why can't I?'

'I agree,' said Gauri, 'men can find love as many times as they want to. Why can't we? But wait a minute . . . are you sure it's love?'

'No, I'm not. All I know is I haven't been able to forget Saveer since I had a talk with him in the pub. And now he doesn't want to recognize me. It made me feel shitty and yet I'm attracted to him.'

Seeing a perfume store, Prisha stopped in her tracks. She went in, followed by her friends. She headed straight to the men's section and smelled every perfume till she found a particular one. She sprayed it on herself a little and some more on her wrist. Then she walked out.

'Finally I know one more thing about him,' she announced, sniffing her wrist. Gauri and Diggy stared at her.

'He wears Pour Homme, Versace.' It sounded like a declaration.

'You sure you aren't the psycho chick kind, right?' Gauri looked at her, wide-eyed.

Prisha gave her a naughty smile. 'I don't know. We discover something new about ourselves every day, don't we?'

Gauri was about to respond but stopped when her phone rang. She excused herself and joined the two a while later.

'I don't know what Sanjeev sir wants,' she said as they made their way towards the exit. 'First he says he doesn't want to stay in touch. When I agree, he gets angry, saying he was only testing me to know if it matters to me if he stops talking to me. Sometimes I think age fucks one's mind up.'

'Could be,' Diggy said.

Prisha, however, had an unlikely reaction.

'What if Saveer is intentionally avoiding me? Maybe he wants to know if I'm really interested in him, or just playing around because he is also the Mean Monster, right?' Her excitement amazed Gauri.

'Mark my words,' Diggy said, 'this girl has lost it.'

By the time they were outside the mall, the trio had divided all work between themselves. Gauri took the responsibility of finishing their respective assignments, while Prisha and Diggy went to the G-Punch office on his two-wheeler. Once there, Prisha sent Diggy to ask if Saveer was inside. He was. They sauntered out. It took them two unbearable hours, three coke cans and two plates of idli from a nearby eatery to finally spot Saveer coming out of his office. Diggy and Prisha high-fived and quickly clambered on to the two-wheeler. Prisha could feel her heart pounding and a sudden rush of blood as they chased Saveer's car. She was thrilled, as if her life had come back to her. If this was what it took to be herself, Prisha thought, she would happily chase Saveer, always.

They tailed his car all the way from his office to Indira Nagar. Saveer parked in front of a house and went inside. Prisha now had a new addition to the list of things she already knew about him: His address.

'Now what? We know where he lives. Do we go inside?' Diggy asked.

Prisha nodded and said, 'That would be an intrusion. I don't want that.'

'Oh, so Miss Psycho chick doesn't like intruding on others. Then what do you want?' Diggy asked sarcastically, removing his helmet and scratching his head.

'I want to invade him.'

'Is there a difference between the two?' Diggy was still scratching his head.

'I don't give a fuck if there's any,' she said, looking up at the house as if she could see what he up to inside.

15

Saveer woke up with a jolt. His forehead was covered in cold sweat. He wiped it with the back of his hand and glanced at the AC—it was on. The dream had unnerved him. He had seen Isha—blood-smeared and her face half-smashed—tiptoe into his bedroom. She caressed his forehead and said she was here to take him with her. Dressed only in his boxers, Saveer got out of the bed and drank some water from a bottle kept on a study table in the room.

He often dreamt about her and every time he would wake up feeling she was in the house, hiding somewhere. Restless, he grabbed a pillow, went downstairs to the living room and collapsed on the couch.

They had decided to move in together in Mumbai even though she had always wanted to settle down in Bengaluru. She was half-Kannadiga and half-Rajput—quite a rare combo.

Back then, he was an investment banker, while she was planning to open her own HR consultancy firm.

They were supposed to get married that year. But he should've known that he would get her killed. Saveer felt a thud in his heart. Just then, the doorbell rang. He looked up at the clock; it was quite late for a visitor to call on him. He walked up to the main door and switched on the video console near it. He couldn't see anybody outside. With slight apprehension, Saveer opened the door. He noticed a square parcel on his doorstep. He picked it up, looked around but couldn't spot anyone. He went back inside.

Saveer ripped opened the parcel to find a skin for his Mac. The skin had a green monster on it with a dialogue box which read: *Don't be so mean to me, Monster*. There was a name underneath: Prisha.

He frowned. It didn't take much long for him to recollect who Prisha was. He was pulled back to the time Isha had parcelled him the power bank.

Did this girl . . . Prisha . . . know about Isha by any chance? Did she try to gain more information about me?

Saveer checked the parcel. There was no address, which meant Prisha had delivered it herself. He slowly folded the skin and dumped it in the trash can. He knew he would have to talk to Prisha once again: the last time. For that, he would have to either wait for her to get to him or . . . Saveer called his assistant.

'Krishna, I want some information on a girl. Prisha Srivastav. Could you get that for me please?'

'Prisha Srivastav, sir? The girl who was admitted by us to the hospital?'

'That's right.'

'When do you want it?'

'ASAP.'

'Please give me few hours, sir.'

'Yes, of course.'

The next morning in office, Krishna knocked on Saveer's cabin. 'Sir, Prisha Srivastav is an eighteen-year-old girl. She is a student of mass communication at Cross University. She stays on BTM Layout. Her number is . . .'

'I only want her address,' Saveer cut him short. He didn't want to meet or talk to her because he had never yelled at a woman in his life and he wanted it keep it that way. After Krishna left, Saveer got back to his work.

In another part of the city, Diggy and Prisha were kissing an irate Gauri's cheeks in the classroom. 'Stop it now!' she yelled. Gauri had completed their assignments the night before and the professor had applauded their efforts in front of the class.

'Gauri deserves a party!' Prisha said happily.

'But I'm broke,' Diggy said. 'Mom is going to send money next week.'

'And the treat is for me, so I'm not going to pitch in,' Gauri said.

Prisha looked disappointed. 'Dad already transferred Rs 12,000 for a new phone,' she murmured.

'Which you instead used to pay our hospital bill. What was the need to do so when they were already paying up?' Diggy sounded cross.

'All right, time for you to know who Prisha really is.' She suddenly sounded determined.

'What do you mean? I already know you are a psycho chick, now what? You are a secret princess as well?' Diggy asked.

'Wait and watch, but first decide where you want to go?'

The three decided to go to Happy Brew in Koramangala right after college.

'Just stay away from me once we are inside till I approach you,' Prisha said.

At Happy Brew, Gauri and Diggy entered as if they were a couple and took a table on the left. They kept their eyes on Prisha who was on the far right, sitting alone. The DJ was warming up to the karaoke night scheduled to begin in the next one hour. Prisha kept staring at him. Soon he caught her eye and flashed a smile. *Not drinking?* He gestured. Prisha nodded and got up. The moment she reached where the DJ was standing, she surprised him with a hug. 'What is this girl up to?' Diggy whispered to Gauri.

'In her words, wait and watch,' Gauri responded.

The moment Prisha felt the DJ's hand on her back, she broke away from the hug. Looking into his eyes, she said, 'You know you remind me of my ex. I'm still in love with him.'

'Aw! Only an idiot can leave a gorgeous girl like you,' he said.

'By the way, I'm Anisha,' she introduced herself.

'I'm Akhil.'

'I know. I follow you on Instagram.'

'Yeah? Wow! You should have DM-ed me.'

'Now I will.' Prisha smiled at him.

'So, no drink?' he asked.

'Umm . . . actually . . . Prisha deliberately mumbled.

'Allow me . . .' he said and shouted to the bartender to put her tab on him.

'Thank you!' Prisha smiled.

'Not a problem. I will be done by 1 a.m.'

'And I shall wait,' she hugged him again and then proceeded to the bar counter. The bartender gave her a pitcher.

'I can't come to the bar again and again. Give me two pitchers,' she said confidently. Even if he was surprised, the bartender didn't betray it. He placed two pitchers in front of her. She took them upstairs, away from Akhil's line of vision. Gauri and Diggy soon joined her—they high-fived each other.

'Are you the same girl who used to sulk around in college at the beginning?' Diggy asked.

'I am. But that wasn't me. This is. I was always this Prisha. That was only what that asshole had turned me into.' With that, the friends clinked their glasses and gulped down the beer. Prisha drank the most.

'What do you guys think, will he like his gift?' Prisha asked. It was sudden question and even if she had given them time to think about it, they wouldn't have been able to answer it.

The DJ announced that the karaoke was about to start. The three scampered down. High and happy, they sang and danced to hearts' content to Eminem, Poets of the Fall, Coldplay and Shakira. And way before 1 a.m., when the DJ was to wind up his gig, Prisha and her posse slunk out of the pub. Once outside, Prisha pulled out her phone only to find twenty missed calls from Zinnia. She called back and was told to get back home immediately.

It was around 12.55 a.m. when Diggy and Gauri dropped her off at her place. Feeling light in the head, Prisha took the stairs even though the elevator was in working order. When she reached her floor, she found the apartment door ajar. Zinnia was sitting in the living room and next to her was a man. Prisha couldn't believe her eyes. The man stood up and said, 'You wanted to see me, right?'

Prisha looked at him for a moment.

'Depends. First, tell me who you are? Saveer Rathod or the Mean Monster?' her words slurred slightly, while she held on to the door for support.

16

Prisha was both scared and confident. She had never experienced such an emotional churn within her before. This was one of those many unprecedented things that the man standing in front of her had made her experience recently. She was yet to unravel or understand some of those feelings. All she had learned thus far was that some feelings are difficult to be attributed to a particular cause. They are also difficult to describe, the meaning of which can itself prove to be elusive.

'Though I know,' Saveer began, 'that you delivered the parcel yourself to my house. I want to know why you would do something like that.'

Prisha tried to focus her alcohol-arrested mind and word a suitable reply. She didn't want to sound stupid.

'I wanted to thank you for helping me.'

'I told you it was my job.'

'Yeah, you told me,' Prisha said and glanced at Zinnia, who was looking at her strictly.

'Then what about the parcel?' Saveer wanted her to come out clean. Did she know more about him than she should have?

'I . . .' Prisha chose her words wisely. 'I like what you told me. I like you.'

Saveer sighed. So it wasn't what he had suspected. Clearly, the girl knew nothing about him. In which case, it was probably his second guess. He walked closer to her. She slowly raised her eyes to look at him. Prisha didn't know what was more damaging: the alcohol or the way their eyes locked on each other.

'Look Prisha, I totally understand being enamoured of someone. Girls and boys usually have a thing for people older to them. Being older, mature might seem sexier at your age. But I must request you to not push this beyond the point it has already reached. I'm thirty-four and you are just a kid in front of me, all right?'

'Kid?' Prisha sounded offended. But she smiled smugly. 'I'm not a fucking kid! You wanna check? Fuck me and I'll give you a child,' she spat at Saveer.

It was so sudden that even Zinnia couldn't hide her embarrassment.

'Prisha!' Zinnia started, but was stopped by Saveer. He looked at Prisha as if he was disappointed and was about to walk out of the flat without another word when Prisha held his hand—the way she had the other night in the pub. He turned around and Prisha let go of him just like last time.

The moment he stepped out of the flat, Zinnia started reprimanding Prisha, but the latter stumbled into her room and collapsed on the bed.

Next day during class-break, Prisha told Gauri about Saveer's surprise visit to her place and all the garbage that she had blurted out in front of him.

'"Fuck you?" Like seriously?' Gauri's jaws dropped. Diggy missed the dramatic turn of events—he had a stomach ache and was recuperating at home.

'I was drunk. But nevertheless.'

The two girls looked at each other and laughed out loud.

'Can I ask you something?' Prisha said.

'Sure.' Gauri sensed an uncomfortable question coming up.

'What is it that makes you hopeful about Sanjeev?' Prisha had been dying to ask her this question for a while now, but couldn't find a good time.

Gauri looked at her. She started tapping on the bench with her fingers.

'Can we go to Nandini's?' she asked in response. Prisha thought that perhaps Gauri didn't want to talk about it. But while sipping tea at Nandini's—the popular eatery in the college campus—she suddenly said: 'Thanks for asking me this. I've been thinking about it. Earlier, I would have had a different answer but then I've realized that I wasn't being honest with myself. I guess we all take time to really be frank to ourselves, especially when it is about something we covet with all our hearts. And after being really honest to myself, I've understood I have a thing for hopelessness.'

'Hopelessness?' Prisha asked.

'I'm pursuing Sanjeev because I think it is a hopeless situation. That he and I will never be together.'

'And that's what you want?'

'No, I don't want that. I have become used to the idea and now I'm enjoying it. That's why I don't do anything to challenge that hopelessness. He asked me to stop contacting him, I did. Then he himself called the other day, so now we are talking again.'

'But that's a pretty dangerous situation to be in.'

'Dangerous is an understatement. I think it's the shittiest situation anybody could ever find themselves in. Just that in my case it is working because Sanjeev doesn't want to be with me the way he is with his wife.'

'And you still love him?' Prisha asked and immediately realized that it was perhaps the most personal question she had ever asked Gauri.

'Prisha,' Gauri said, 'I don't come from a normal family like you or Diggy. I've a stepmother and a stepfather now for the past two years. I have grown up seeing my biological parents fight like dogs all the time, telling me I was a mistake.' There was a long pause. Prisha didn't know if she should say something. She was already feeling guilty having asked her questions about her relationship with Sanjeev.

Eventually, Gauri spoke again. 'Sanjeev is my first relationship with a man. Now whenever he fucks me and calls it love, I want to believe it desperately. Even though before or after the so-called lovemaking sessions, I very well know that he is bluffing. But I guess when the fact that you're a mistake is hardwired in your psyche since childhood, even a false claim of being loved makes you clutch at that straw with all your life.'

She didn't say anything after that. Nor did Prisha. The two attended three more lectures, during which neither spoke a word to each other.

Gauri's words weighed heavily on Prisha. After coming back from college, she made some tea for herself, while turning over Gauri's words in her mind. 'Hopelessness in a relationship.' Was she heading towards that? The perfect way to screw up her life. Saveer's elusiveness, his refusal to feel for her the same way she felt for him was pulling her even more towards him. She wanted to know him more and was perhaps open to the idea of being led to wherever she would be after knowing him. But she couldn't be Gauri. She couldn't be in love with the hopelessness that Saveer seemed to represent at that moment. After the open declaration of her interest in him the night before, he could have fucked her on the pretext that he liked her as well—the way Sanjeev had done with Gauri. But he did not. He tried to explain why they were not right for each other, even if it was with a bogus excuse of age difference. And he was a guy known to give women unprecedented sexual pleasures! The inherent contradiction in him, just like his alpha male confidence, aggression, even his patronizing tone, was way too sexy to be taken casually. Prisha knew she was attracted to him, but couldn't understand the nature of this attraction. Was it just a crush? A rebound? Or was it something deeper? What if it was ... *love*? She could only know the answer once she knew more about him.

Hope is what makes one refuse to give up on a journey. Without hope, like Gauri was, it would just be an unending loop: Sanjeev would come, fuck her and leave. And as Gauri had herself admitted, she knew all about it but didn't want to look for an alternative. *But I have to find an alternative*, Prisha thought. *I can't just get Saveer gifts, gain his attention and revel in it.* A sudden restlessness made her pace up and down her room. She realized she had made a mistake by getting to know the Mean Monster before coming closer to Saveer. She should have gone about it the other way round.

Prisha came out of her room to find Zinnia watching TV on the couch. She was in the exact position as Prisha had seen her in when she had come back home an hour ago.

'Zin, how did you track down the Mean Monster?' Prisha asked. Zinnia's was flipping through the channels. She put the remote down and said, 'Not again, Prisha. Please!'

'I'm asking you about the Mean Monster and not Saveer. I too want to be fucked by him,' Prisha said.

Zinnia sat up looking at her intently.

89

17

Prisha learnt that there was no pattern in Saveer's appearance as the Mean Monster. He had remained untraceable solely by randomly selecting his women. There was a phone number, which was circulated far and wide, along with details of his sexual prowess. Prisha racked her brains to think of a way to get through to the Mean Monster. Unfortunately, her friends weren't of much help. No matter how much they tried, it was nearly impossible to guess when and where the Mean Monster would make his next appearance.

A fortnight later, Zinnia told Prisha that a girl in one of her WhatsApp groups was boasting about an impending night with him.

'Please put me in touch with her.'

'I don't think it is a good idea. You won't be able to handle him, sweets,' Zinnia said.

Prisha had divulged only stray pieces of information to Zinnia about what had transpired between Saveer and her. Zinnia was under the impression that Prisha was just lusting after Saveer and she intended to keep it that way.

'Trying it once won't kill me,' Prisha said.

Zinnia realized that trying to coax her out of it was going to be a futile effort. So she connected her to Kriti, the Mean Monster's upcoming date. Prisha cooked up a super-emotional, fake story about an imaginary friend who had two problems: one, she was suffering from cancer, and second, she was a virgin. Prisha, since she was her best friend, wanted to request the Mean Monster to let her friend experience an orgasm before cancer sucked the life out of her. Prisha made her story as dramatic as possible. She knew that bullshit, if sold well, could also have takers. By the end of it, Kriti was moved to tears. When she recovered, she said: 'I really appreciate your sentiments for your bestie but I've been trying to track this guy down since the last three months. So I don't think I will be able to let go of him just like that. I'm sorry.'

Prisha asked her if she could lead the Mean Monster to some place where she could talk to him after they were done.

'What if I step in after you guys are done? Like, do you have a place in mind where you want to do him?'

Kriti shook her head. 'I stay in a PG where men aren't allowed.'

'Then?'

'He told me it would either be in his car or at a hotel, since I don't have my own place.'

'Could you please push him for the car as a hotel might be a bit tricky for me?'

Kriti kept looking at Prisha. *She looks like a teenager*, she thought, *and her plan sounds weird.* Yet when she remembered the part about cancer, she felt Prisha was doing what any good friend would have done.

'I think I can do that,' Kriti said. Prisha gave her a tight hug.

At the scheduled time the following weekend, Prisha was ready and sitting behind Diggy on his two-wheeler. The plan was simple. They would follow the couple in the car and stop a few metres behind them. The moment Kriti got out of the car, excusing herself to pee, Prisha would approach Saveer. She would tell him that she wasn't a high-on-hormone teenager who was happy gifting him stuff and being a secret admirer. And if he had anything on his mind, he should tell her straight.

Saveer stopped the car again on a dark, deserted stretch on the Mysore highway.

'I swear we would have had to stop for a refill if he had gone further,' Diggy said while switching off the engine of the scooty.

However, the wait was more challenging than the pursuit. They waited from 11 p.m. to 12.45 a.m. Diggy even dozed off in between but not Prisha. She was trying hard not to think of what was going on inside the car. Somewhere deep down, she felt uncomfortable thinking what the two of them must be up to. She could feel the colour rising in her cheeks. When the door finally opened, Prisha could feel her breath quickening.

'I hate to say this but I've to pee. Can you please excuse me for a few seconds?' Kriti said.

She looked around for Prisha and saw her in the distance, walking towards the car. Taking her cue, she disappeared into the darkness nearby.

Prisha went and tapped on the window. Saveer was buttoning up his shirt. He looked up.

'You!' he sounded furious. He threw the car door open and jumped out.

'Have you been following me? Don't tell me you still didn't get what I told you?' Saveer said through gritted teeth.

'I'm glad you didn't ask who I am.' Prisha had a foolish smile pasted on her face.

'You think this is some sort of a joke?' Saveer tried hard not to raise his voice.

'You think an eighteen-year-old girl, following a thirty-four-year-old man out of city limits and on to the highway at this ungodly hour could possibly be a joke?'

'What do you want!'

Prisha wasn't ready for this. She had too many things on her mind.

'Your words . . .'

'I understand you were moved by them but what next?' Saveer was running out of patience.

'I want to know more about you.' That best summed up what Prisha wanted from him. Saveer looked into her eyes. He could tell by looking into them how weak she could possibly be.

'I'm going to say this once,' he whispered. 'STAY AWAY FROM ME! I'm not a good guy. Just. Stay. Away.' And with that he turned to get into the car. 'But . . .' Prisha tried again.

Saveer turned around in a flash. 'I killed my girlfriend five years ago. Literally. I kill anyone who gets to know me. Or comes close to me. And I am not joking,' he lashed out at her. If till then, Saveer's pupils had been a liquid pool of unending darkness, Prisha observed that a spark of guilt now lit up in them and his face contorted as if he was feeling acute remorse. But it lasted for hardly a fraction of a second before Saveer checked himself.

'I'm sorry, but are you guys done?' It was Kriti. 'I can't stay alone in the darkness anymore.'

Saveer understood that the two girls were together in the fiasco. He climbed back into the car and started the engine. Kriti slipped in beside him quietly and in no time, the car was just a dot in the horizon. For a while, Prisha stood rooted to her spot, still absorbing all that had happened in the last couple of minutes. At that moment, Saveer had become like an unputdownable book, a page-turner.

Diggy came up behind her on his two-wheeler, yawning. He had missed the scene. 'What happened?' he asked, sounding bored and sleepy. 'What did he say?'

'That he is a killer.'

Diggy's eyes flew open as Prisha narrated what Saveer had told her.

By the time they reached home, it was almost dawn. Diggy updated Gauri and both of them demanded more information from Prisha, who was unusually quiet. The other two sat with her, waiting for her to break her silence, but dozed off in no time.

In the stillness of the early morning, she googled Saveer's name along with the keywords 'killer', 'murderer', 'girlfriend', 'police case', but nothing turned up. She concluded that it must have been a bluff to get rid of her.

At around six in the morning, she sat down in Gauri's study with swollen eyes, intending to write something on a pad, knowing fully well what her next—and last—step would be. A teardrop fell on the pad. She stared at the pool of transparent liquid and realized that it contained a world within it, which she wasn't yet ready to part with.

18

Prisha took a deep breath as she found herself standing outside the G-Punch office. Then she walked right in. Ignoring the receptionist, she pushed open the glass door and stepped into the area where people were busy working on their desktops. She turned right and barged into Saveer's cabin. He was typing something on his laptop. The receptionist came running after her.

'I need five minutes. That's all,' Prisha pleaded. Saveer studied her and then gestured to the receptionist to leave.

'What is it?' he asked.

Prisha handed him a note. 'I'm more coherent when I write down anything. I just want you to read it in front of me. I'll leave right after.'

Saveer took the note, opened it, peered at her over his spectacles, and started reading.

From the time you told me about Complete Love, I got lost in its concept. I couldn't help but think, not only about it, but also about you. What made you discover it? Most importantly, I too wanted to experience it. It felt as if I was imploring you to teach me a skill, like swimming, that I didn't have. It was after days of mulling over the feeling that you had brewed inside me that I finally understood what it was that you had done that made me fall head over heels for you. You made me unlearn, Saveer. Love is so tricky. I know you may already know this but take for instance these two words: coronation and corrosion. They might sound similar but have very different meanings. I thought my last relationship was an emotional coronation of sorts . . . but guess what? I realized with bitter experience that it was actually a corrosion . . . of my naivety. The realization was so scary. You invest your time in a relationship, nurturing it, only to witness it withering, rotting. Then where do you go? How do you even restart? Emotional injuries are the worst, aren't they? They have a mind of their own and simply refuse to listen to you. Anyway, enough with the blabber.

The point is, it was you and your words which helped me heal. You helped me unlearn my past, helped me stop wallowing and get over and past Utkarsh, my ex. You prevented me from regretting mourning the death of such a relationship at a later stage of my life. I truly feel free now and am ready for fresh imprints. The next time may or may not be forever, but I want to thank you for helping me get over Utkarsh. He had made me feel terrible at the end of our relationship. Although I don't know much about life, I think very few men can make a girl feel like that.

You said you had killed your girlfriend. For some reason, I just cannot bring myself to believe it.

Saveer sighed, folded the letter and looked up at her.

'Goodbye, Mr Rathod. It was a pleasure knowing you and not knowing you at the same time,' Prisha said in a choked voice. She didn't wait for him to respond.

Once outside, she couldn't help but break down. Prisha had witnessed a different facet of—for the lack of a better word—love, where one yearns for another person but knows he or she can't be had. Two roads branched out in front of her: the road to acceptance and the road to self-destruction.

Saveer reread the letter in the privacy of his cabin. Suddenly, a business mail popped up on his screen. He folded Prisha's letter and kept it inside his pocket before clicking on it. The rest of the day went by with Saveer somehow feeling stifled. He skipped lunch.

In the evening when he reached home, he switched on Mean Monster's number. He generally maintained a decent time gap between his hook-ups, but this time he hardly let a day pass. He tried not to think much. There were several messages from women. Mostly old, but some new. He randomly messaged a few. Couple of them responded saying they were free and interested. Saveer zeroed in on one. She wanted to meet at the Sky Lounge.

While riding his bike to the lounge, Saveer wondered how lonely a life he was used to. It would sound unbelievable to people: no parents, no siblings, no cousins, no friends, no bestie, no pet and certainly no love interest. Yet, he had had all of them once upon a time. Everyone, including his dog Piano, was dead now. Every time he lost a loved one, he felt wary of starting a new relationship. It had been nine years since Piano had died but Saveer had never had the courage to adopt another dog. Saveer as Mean Monster was an example of how good he was at creating a bubble around himself, where he led a sequestered, shadowy life. The Monster's exploits were Saveer's attempts at emotional self-flagellation. The means were different for different people but that's how one moved on after a heartbreak. If Saveer had not convinced himself that he was a bad person by randomly hooking up with women he didn't know, he wouldn't have been able to move on after Isha's death. This was darker than mere guilt because it involved a deliberate and painful attempt at manipulating one's own existence.

Saveer reached Sky Lounge on time. Compared to other nights, he was more aggressive and impatient to have sex. However, he wasn't seeking to satiate his hunger for sex but an opportunity to punish himself for Isha's death.

It took him twenty minutes to get over the hi-hello and get to the point. He had booked a room in the Hyatt. Once inside the room, the girl wanted to talk to him but he told her he was on a deadline. So, they got into bed and stripped. He pushed himself into her. Twenty minutes later, he was out. While the girl lay in bed, waiting for her breath to steady, Saveer went to the washroom. This had been the Mean Monster's shortest performance to date.

Prisha's words kept coming back to him especially the part where she had said that he had helped her unlearn.

He stood in front of the mirror, without looking at his reflection. He turned on the tap, blocked the sink and let the water accumulate. When the washbasin was full, he dunked his head in it.

Saveer understood that perhaps Prisha was nursing a similar wound, although the intensity was different. She could heal but he couldn't. Or maybe he didn't want to. He loved Isha and possibly didn't want to part with her memories yet. He wasn't ready to be with anyone else.

How could he unlearn what life had taught him? That everything had an expiry date, that no form of love was permanent. That no matter how many promises you made to your loved ones, *forever is a lie*. Saveer lifted up his head and took a few short breaths. He ran his fingers through his hair and then impulsively smashed the mirror in front of him.

'What happened, baby?' the girl called out from the bedroom.

Saveer didn't respond. He washed his hand, which was bloodied and got dressed.

'Are you leaving already?' the girl asked.

'Everything will be paid. You can leave in the morning if you want to.'

'Thanks, baby.'

Saveer turned to look at her. 'Don't call me baby.' He banged the door shut after him.

He drove his bike faster than usual, tears blinding him. He stopped at Nandi Hills and parked his bike at the edge of a cliff. He yelled out Isha's name as if she would hear him and come hug him tight and tell him he'd been having a nightmare. Saveer knelt down. Prisha's letter had pushed him to the edge.

How do I unlearn you, Isha? Saveer mumbled and started sobbing loudly.

He sat in silence till his tears dried up. It was slightly chilly but he was oblivious to it.

Suddenly, there was a loud noise. He turned around to find his bike on the road. He frowned. In the upturned bike's headlight, he saw a silhouette . . . of a woman in a salwar kameez. He stood up and rubbed his eyes. The woman stepped back. Saveer rushed to his bike. There was nobody. Did he imagine the woman? Was he hallucinating?

19

Why is she sitting alone? Why not with us? Diggy WhatsApped Gauri. They were in class. The classroom was semi-dark, a slide show presentation in progress.

Something's up. And she isn't telling us about it, Gauri replied. They were sitting next to each other but Prisha was in a corner. Gauri tried to ask her but just then the professor entered the class. She waited for the lecture to get over. Then she approached Prisha. 'What's up? Why are you avoiding us?'

'I'm not. I'm not feeling well.'

'Periods?'

'No.'

'Then?'

'Nothing?'

'Did Saveer say anything?' Diggy joined them. Prisha shook her head. They sat beside her, waiting for the next class to begin.

'Can I have your house keys please?' Prisha said.

Gauri looked at her for a moment and said, 'You can tell us if there's something bothering you.'

'I'm feeling sleepy. And Zinnia isn't there.'

'What about your set of keys?' Diggy asked.

'I forgot them,' Prisha lied. Zinnia was at home and she wanted to avoid her. Or for that matter any other person.

Gauri gave her the keys. Prisha stood up, thanked her and walked out of the class.

'Do you think she is being honest?' Diggy asked.

'No.'

'Why would she lie? And that too to us?'

Gauri had an inkling but refrained from saying anything. They stood up as the professor came inside.

It was evening by the time Gauri and Diggy reached home. At first, they rang the bell for a while, hoping that Prisha would open the door. When she didn't, they let themselves in using Diggy's set of keys. They found Prisha curled up on the mattress in Gauri's room, totally sloshed, an empty bottle of Old Monk lying next to her.

'Oh shit!' Gauri exclaimed and rushed to her side. Prisha's cheeks were kohl-stained. It was obvious that she had been crying. Gauri pulled her head on to her lap and slapped her gently, asking, 'Can you hear me, Prisha? Wake up!' Diggy sat down beside them, nervous.

'Did she drink the whole bottle?' he asked.

'Seems like it. We didn't have any spare ones. Prisha! Prisha!'

Prisha tried to open her eyes and move a bit. She couldn't recognize where she was. Gauri slapped her a few more times.

103

'Get some water,' Gauri told Diggy. He scampered off to the kitchen.

'Gauri, my friend,' Prisha slurred, 'I want him.'

'Who?'

'That stupid Monster. I want him.' Prisha held on to Gauri's arms and dozed off in no time.

'What did she say?' Diggy had come back with a glass of water.

'Nothing. We have to do something. I know how it is. It starts with one bottle and soon you become an addict. Like I have.' Gauri laid Prisha's head down on the mattress and stood up.

'So, she said something,' Diggy was quick to infer.

'Hmm, she did.'

'What?'

'We'll have to meet Saveer,' Gauri said after some thought.

'Why would she want us to meet him?'

'She doesn't. I think we should.'

'And tell him what?'

'Just keep supporting me in whatever I say, okay?'

'Okay.'

Gauri quickly took a few clicks of a sloshed Prisha. Diggy had no idea why she did that.

Convinced that Prisha would be asleep, the two locked the flat from outside and went to the G-Punch office. Saveer didn't exactly remember who they were until they sat down in front of him and introduced themselves. They had managed an appointment with him on the pretext of a college project.

'We are Prisha's friends,' Gauri said. She tried to be confident but only she knew how hard her heart was pounding. She wanted Saveer to say yes to what she had in mind.

'I think that thing is done with. She had said she wouldn't be bothering me again,' Saveer said.

'She won't. But she is bothering herself. She drank an entire bottle of rum and was blabbering your name constantly,' Gauri said.

'I think you should inform her parents.'

'I don't know what it was like when you were eighteen, but we don't involve our parents in such things,' Gauri said.

'Okay. Your call. But what can I do?'

'See, it is pretty obvious that she has a crush on you. And as you know very well, crushing is temporary. It goes away the moment you get to know the person a little. But the pricier a crush acts, the person infatuated becomes all the more smitten. Do you get it?'

He nodded, maintaining his poise.

'Thanks. All I'm saying is, please, don't be so harsh on her.'

'Please, sir,' Diggy spoke up for the first time. He had to support Gauri as planned.

'I don't think we are meeting again so there is no question of being harsh,' Saveer responded coldly.

'I would request you to meet her.'

'Why would I meet her?'

'May I show you something?' Gauri asked, unlocking her phone.

Saveer nodded. She went around to where Saveer was sitting and showed him Prisha's pictures.

'If you meet her, it would help her stop crushing and behave normally. Then even if you tell her to stay away, she will do so without the Old Monk.'

'Please,' Diggy pleaded.

Gauri's plan sounded plain stupid to Saveer.

'It has happened to me too. I had a crush on this guy but the moment he started talking, I got over him.'

'What if I say I don't have time for this?'

'Of course, you don't. But I'm requesting you to make some. Prisha may end up wasting her life, not studying and turning into a full-time alcoholic. Do you really want that on your hands? You who runs an NGO for the safety of women.' Gauri was on a roll.

'Would you really, sir?' Diggy echoed. Gauri glared at him.

Saveer smirked at the way Gauri had dragged in morality into the conversation. He had a choice. And he chose to end this the best way possible. For him and for her.

'What do you guys study?' he asked.

'We are mass communication students at Cross University.'

'You have a bright future. You are good at convincing people.'

'Thank you,' Diggy said.

'Does that mean . . .' Gauri started. She was interrupted by a knock on the door.

'Come in,' Saveer said.

A lean man entered with a laptop in his hands. He went across to Saveer and showed him something. Saveer looked at it and then turned towards Gauri, 'G-Punch is looking for young content writing interns for our social media pages. Do you think you guys can be of some use?'

Gauri's face lit up. 'I can confirm three names,' she said.

'Good,' Saveer said and turned to the man, 'Make them sit with Mayank for the budget we have and other paperwork.'

'Sure sir,' the man said. He went out, followed by Diggy.

'I can't thank you enough,' Gauri said, before leaving.

'Not a problem. Ask her not to drink. It's not a good thing. Not now, not ever.'

'Sure I will.'

Once done with the paperwork—they would get a stipend of Rs 10,000 each—Diggy was over the moon.

'I always wanted to earn!'

'Same here. No more asking money from parents all the time.'

They hugged each other.

'But tell me something, why did you have to presume that he is Prisha's crush? Maybe she really loves him. Why did you have to decide that?' Diggy asked, sounding concerned.

'Duffer, I know she loves him.'

'Then?'

'I've a plan. So don't ask questions,' Gauri said and climbed on to the two-wheeler. Diggy got up on the pillion seat, excited, knowing well that when Gauri had a plan, it rarely went wrong.

20

When Prisha woke up the next day, she couldn't believe her eyes after Gauri showed her the internship offer from G-Punch.

'How did this happen?' she asked, reading the agreement carefully. She kept looking at Gauri incredulously while flipping through the papers.

They were in Gauri's room. Diggy was still asleep. 'Well, I found their sponsored ad on Facebook. Told Diggy about it and we applied. When we were told they had three vacancies, we filled in your name as well. Now don't tell me you won't go.'

Prisha put the agreement down. 'You think I should?'

'Of course. In fact, the timings are flexible. We won't miss our lectures. We can go to office if we want to, else we can just mail them the content.'

'You know I'm not concerned about that.'

'Hmm. Then why don't you want to be close to Saveer?'

Prisha paused before answering, 'I had told him I won't ever bother him again.'

'Why would you say that?'

'I didn't want to come across as clingy. Moreover, he has an issue.'

'What issue?'

'He said he had killed his girlfriend. I googled but couldn't find anything on the Internet about it. So, I don't know if he was bluffing.'

'He killed his girlfriend,' Gauri asked rhetorically and seemed thoughtful. 'He has to be bluffing!'

At that moment, Prisha's phone rang. It was her mother. She talked to her for a few minutes. When she joined Gauri again, the latter said, 'Why don't you try to befriend him first?' This was part of Gauri's plan of bringing Saveer and Prisha together.

'Maybe he doesn't open up to anyone just like that,' she continued, realizing Prisha was considering the option.

'And you think this content writing stint would be the right excuse to befriend him?'

'Why not? I know you have feelings for him.'

Gauri is right, Prisha realized. She did have feelings for him. She didn't know when the pursuit had become so serious. In fact, she had problem wondering if there really was a time when she didn't have any feelings for him. But why? It was funny how the past blurs when someone is in love. It feels like there was never a before, or an after. The person makes you believe that the present is both the journey and the destination. Both the cause and the effect.

'I think to know him more is the best I can do,' Prisha said feeling jittery and wondering how she could possibly face Saveer again after saying goodbye to him.

Prisha had to sign the offer. So Gauri dropped her at the G-Punch office but refused to accompany her inside.

'You go, I need to meet Sanjeev in the next lane. Call me once you're done,' Gauri said. Prisha nodded and went inside. The receptionist connected her to the person concerned who helped her finish the paperwork. She was allotted a seat, where she switched on her laptop. A senior employee at the office explained her job and gave her, her first assignment. Prisha messaged Gauri that she would spend the rest of the day in office and would bunk college. *I will be with Sanjeev till you are done*, came her response.

It was just before lunch when Saveer came out of his cabin. He noticed Prisha on her laptop, typing furiously. He went over to where she was sitting.

'You can do this at home as well. You don't have to bunk college.'

Prisha looked up and realized it was *him*. 'I don't have any important class today.'

Saveer gave her an acknowledging nod and went outside. She went to Abhay Kumar, the man who had helped her find a seat, and asked, 'Does he always leave this early?'

'No! He is usually the last person to leave. He is going out for lunch.'

'Home?'

'Nope. There's a restaurant nearby where he goes daily.'

'Which one?'

'Ishanvi's. He is the owner.'

'Okay!' Prisha said, impressed. She wanted to follow him but it would have been too obvious. What if he got angry with her on her very first day? Prisha decided to call Gauri and the two went to Forum Mall for a bite and a movie.

She completed her assignment and sent it on time the next day. Gauri and Diggy had also started their internships. For the next two days, Prisha couldn't skip college. She would attend classes during the day and finish her office assignment at night. On the third day, she bunked college again and went to G-Punch.

She sat with the laptop open in front of her but her eyes were fixed on Saveer's cabin. She kept telling herself that he would step out any minute. And he did, to get some coffee from a beverage dispenser outside. Prisha thanked her stars for making him a caffeine addict, or else she wouldn't have got to see him much. She didn't miss a single opportunity to be close to him. Every time, Saveer went to get coffee, so did Prisha—and she wasn't even a big fan of caffeine. Once Saveer left, she would stash the cup and go back to her seat. In between all the caffeine-induced meet-ups, their eyes would often meet. For Prisha, these moments were akin to sharing small yet significant conversations with Saveer. They were like spring to those buds inside her, which she wasn't sure would ever bloom. And now they did, one lovely petal at a time.

The next day she had an important class but Prisha wasn't able to focus. She went to office along with Gauri and Diggy. She didn't want to come across as too obvious about her intentions, or too desperate. During lunch, Gauri and Diggy decided to go to college; they would give her proxy. Prisha, in the meantime, followed Saveer to Ishanvi's. A few of her colleagues were there as well. So Prisha's presence didn't seem too calculated.

The restaurant was two hundred metres from the office. Standing at the entrance, she noticed Saveer sitting in a corner. There were other people too. A staffer came and welcomed her inside. The moment she stepped in, she realized Saveer's eyes were on her. It made her nervous. She pretended as if she was looking for a seat. Then she noticed Saveer waving his hand. She didn't know what to do—should she pretend to be surprised, or avoid looking at him? The waiter standing behind her said, 'Ma'am, I think sir is calling you.'

Prisha looked at Saveer and gave him a forced smile. She went over to where he was sitting.

'You can join me if you are alone and comfortable,' he said. Prisha sat down opposite him.

'Thanks,' she said. She noticed he was having a salad.

'It's okay,' Saveer said and gave her the menu. Prisha's hands shook as she opened it. Nothing was making sense to her. She could feel herself clamming up with every passing moment.

'I'll have some soup,' she said. Saveer gestured to a waiter.

'One Chef's Special soup, please.'

'Right,' the waiter took down the order and left. Saveer turned to look at Prisha, only to find her gulp down an entire glass of water.

'You want more?' he asked.

Prisha shook her head. It was the first time Saveer had talked normally to her. But why?

She knew his eyes were on her, which made her look elsewhere. She looked everywhere except at him. Her heart was pounding. She had never been this nervous before, not even when she had had sex for the first time.

'You've got a call,' Saveer said. For a moment, Prisha didn't understand. Saveer pointed towards her phone, which was kept on the table. It was on silent mode. Her mother was calling.

'Hi, Mumma. Yeah, I'm in college only,' Prisha said, stealing a glance at Saveer. 'I had my lunch. Yes, will go home straight. Don't worry. I will call you later. Bye.' She cut the line.

The way Prisha talked to her mother, made Saveer miss his parents.

'Where do your parents stay?' he asked.

'Faridabad. And yours?'

'They are no more.'

'Oh! I'm sorry to hear that,' she said. The mention of death made her recall how he had told her that he had killed his girlfriend. Should she ask him about it?

'Are you from Bengaluru?' she asked.

Saveer shook his head, 'No, I'm from Jodhpur in Rajasthan but I have studied in New Delhi and London. I worked as an investment banker in Hong Kong and then in Mumbai. Made loads of money at a young age, travelled a lot too. Now I stay here, running G-Punch, Ishanvi's and a small ambulance service for highway emergencies called First Call.'

'Why Bengaluru?'

Saveer paused and said, 'Someone wanted to settle down here.'

'Who?' Prisha blurted out before she could stop herself.

'Never mind.'

Prisha understood that it had to be his girlfriend. *Dead girlfriend*, she corrected herself. A man who had settled in an unknown city simply because his ex-girlfriend had wanted him to? She wanted to touch Saveer to tell herself he was real and not a figment of her imagination.

The waiter came and served Prisha the Chef's Special soup. She sprinkled some salt and pepper in it and had a spoonful.

'How are you now?'

Prisha didn't understand.

'The first time we met, you were crying because of a break-up. If it makes you uncomfortable then don't answer.'

'I met someone who taught me what a fool I was crying over something so worthless,' Prisha said, focusing on her soup.

Saveer understood whom she was referring to. He smiled.

'May I ask you something?' she said. Saveer nodded.

'The way you uttered those four words . . .'

'Which ones?'

'Forever is a lie. I want to know why you said so. Do you really believe in it?'

Saveer wiped his mouth with the napkin, kept it aside and said, 'I had read somewhere about the saddest word in the dictionary. You know what it is?'

Prisha nodded.

'The word *almost*. I *almost* had a good life. I *almost* had a family. I *almost* had friends. I *almost* had love in my life. I *almost* . . .' He paused. 'Had her.' He sounded forlorn.

'Excuse me,' he said abruptly and walked out of the restaurant.

Prisha went back to office after finishing her soup but didn't see Saveer for the rest of the day. She kept turning over the word *almost* in her mind. She too *almost* had Utkarsh. She couldn't bear another situation where she *almost* had someone. She would *have* that someone,

Prisha promised herself. Saveer was reserved but she would make him open up in front of her. And for that, even if she had to come across as someone pushy, she would do that.

Around five in the evening, Prisha waited outside for Saveer to come out. When he did, she intentionally bumped into him, pretending it to be a coincidence.

'Going home?' she asked.

'Yeah. Aren't you?'

'My battery is dead and I can't book a cab for myself. And I don't rely on autorickshaws. So wondering what to do,' she left the sentence hanging, hoping he would understand what she hinting at.

'Let me drop you home,' he offered. Prisha wanted to jump with joy but calmed herself down and said, 'Umm, okay.' She got into his car.

'Don't you play music while driving?' she asked as they reached the first traffic signal.

'I like listening to instrumental music at home,' he answered.

'Hmm.' Sadly, Prisha wasn't into instrumental.

'What do you do on weekends?' she asked. He stared at her.

'I meant when you aren't the Mean Monster.'

Saveer was quiet. Prisha realized that perhaps he wasn't enjoying the Q and A session.

'Okay, one last question before you decide never to drop me home again . . .'

Saveer had a faint smile on his face.

'Doesn't it bother you when you hook up randomly? I tried it once but realized I'll never be able to do it again.'

Saveer changed the gear rather abruptly. Prisha was trying to keep the conversation going but something told her it had been the wrong question to ask. She was about to apologize when Saveer said, 'What bothers me is I won't ever be able to feel her presence again. Never ever.'

Prisha knew he was referring to his dead girlfriend— the one he claimed to have killed. She desperately wanted to know the details. Did she cheat on him and hence he killed her? Did he go to jail for it? Did he . . . there were so many questions but she knew it would be rude to ask him anything right now. She had to get closer to him so that he would open up with prodding.

'First, you have a life-changing experience. You immerse yourself in it, become invested and then life tells you, rather abruptly, that what you were experiencing so far was just an illusion. And you are to live with that realization, which is why I told you forever is a lie. So is everything else that leads us towards such a lie.'

Prisha looked at him in surprise. This had never happened with Utkarsh. Every time she met Saveer, Prisha felt as if she was growing a bit more. It was almost as if she could feel her wings being shaped, one feather at a time. As if she were a stone slab and Saveer's thoughts chiselled her mind, revealing her true self. They reached her place. Saveer parked the car outside the lane since there was already an SUV there. Prisha got down and was surprised to see him follow suit.

'I'll walk you to the gate,' he said. It was a quiet walk but each time her hand brushed against his, accidentally, it was like dropping pebbles in a half-filled bowl of water, stirring up her emotions from somewhere deep within.

They reached the gate of her apartment.

'Take care, bye,' she said.

'Bye.'

Saveer turned to walk back to his car when he felt someone holding his hand. He turned around. Prisha placed a quick peck on his cheek.

'I just wanted to thank you,' she said and went inside her apartment.

Saveer stood there for a few seconds. After a long time, a kiss hadn't reeked of lust. It was a wet peck. He rubbed his cheek and walked back to his car. *Her friend was right*, he thought. This young girl had a going-weak-in-the-knees kind of crush on him. And it would ebb away, he knew. Only love never ebbs away, not until it snatches you from yourself. He drove back home.

As he stepped inside the house, the living room lit up. He headed straight for his bedroom. However, on the staircase, much to his horror, he found scattered, broken pieces of all the photographs of Isha and him.

21

Saveer picked up the broken pieces. He was careful not to step on a shard of glass. He looked around. There was nobody. He checked the windows and the main door again. There were no signs of a forced entry. He went to the kitchen, the bedroom, the terrace: everything was exactly the way he had left it. He decided to order fresh frames for the photographs. He didn't understand how the photographs had fallen down. When he couldn't think of a rational explanation, he dismissed the incident from his mind and took a shower, followed by a quiet dinner. The kiss kept coming back to him but he decided to distract himself. Putting on a raga by Ustaad Amjad Ali Khan, Saveer went off to sleep.

Meanwhile, Prisha understood that with Saveer, things would progress slowly. She would have to be patient and careful. From whatever little she deciphered of him, he, unlike her, seemed to have bottled up his emotions. And perhaps his ex-girlfriend had a big role to play in it. He had told her that he killed her. Prisha desperately wanted to know what he meant. *Was it just his way of warding me off? Was it symbolical or . . .* she also knew she would have to earn his trust. And friendship was the best way to become a part of someone without running the risk of being labelled as an emotional intruder.

From the next day onwards, every time Prisha went to office, she made sure that she bumped into Saveer. She wanted to have lunch with him every day but his aloofness made it a little awkward for her to approach him. But she was determined. From the security guard outside to his personal assistant—she sought out everyone in office to inquire about him. She couldn't dig out much on him except for two things. Firstly, that his ex-girlfriend's name was Ishanvi, which she had already guessed from the name of his restaurant, and secondly, it wasn't her name on his caller tune. The latter she discovered one day when she trailed him to the coffee machine and his phone rang—*I love you Isha.*

She was mistaken. When she had heard it the first time at Nandi Hills, she was intrigued. After learning the truth, she wished she had never heard it at all. It made her uncomfortable to realize just how much he loved Isha, still.

Prisha updated her work status—content writer at G-Punch—on Facebook. Her mother was the first one to inquire about it.

'It is just an internship, Mumma. Every student does it,' she said. Her mother didn't want her to waste time not studying. But she didn't ask her anything else once Prisha said it was her college that had arranged the internship. The next one to inquire was Zinnia.

'You never told me!' she accused her when Prisha got back home.

'I joined a week ago,' Prisha lied, even though it was close to a month since she had joined G-Punch.

'Isn't that where Saveer works?' Zinnia sensed something fishy.

'Yeah, he owns it.'

Zinnia smiled slyly.

'Now come on, don't hide it from me.'

'Hide what, Zin?'

'He is the fucking Mean Monster and you are working for him. Don't tell me nothing has happened.'

Prisha felt an instant jolt. She didn't understand why.

'I'm not really interested in him anymore. This was purely coincidental. Excuse me,' she said and went to her room. It took her three days to understand why she had experienced that jolt. Zinnia had known him sexually whereas she hadn't. It wasn't like she was seeking a strictly sexual relationship with him and yet it disturbed her.

'What do you think of sex?' she asked Gauri. They were taking a break while completing their college assignment at Gauri's place. Diggy was out shopping groceries.

'It's good,' Gauri said. She was scrolling through her Instagram feed.

'No, I mean is it very important?'

'Of course, it is.' Gauri noticed that Prisha looked lost.

'If you have something specific in mind, you can tell me about it.'

'Can there be a relationship without any sexual impulses?' Prisha asked.

'You think Saveer isn't interested?'

'Just answer me, Gauri.'

'I don't know what could be the right answer to that. Love, sex, everything is so screwed up. Almost everything I hear or read about sex or love sounds as if people say it without really believing in it. Like people only want to sound intelligent while defining love or sex. Nobody has any idea what's the real deal.'

'You really think so?'

'Okay, once Sanjeev was trying to explain the concept of soulmates and he said an individual soul in itself is too handicapped to feel anything. It is like an empty matchbox. It is only when it finds a matchstick in the form of another soul that there's light, revealing one's own dark corners to oneself. That's the purpose of a soulmate.'

Prisha took some time to absorb what Gauri had said.

'Pardon me, I thought you guys have a strictly sexual relationship. At least as far as he is concerned,' she said.

'Well, he told me all those things after he had fucked me for hours.'

123

Prisha was taken aback.

'That's the thing with older men,' Gauri said, 'especially intellectual ones. They are always full of amazing thoughts, which makes the sex even better.'

The girls laughed.

'I want to confess,' Prisha said, 'or else it will continue to disturb me. I want to move in with you guys.'

'Anything wrong with Zinnia?'

Prisha nodded. 'She has slept with Saveer. So . . .'

'I understand. You're most welcome.'

'Thank you so much.' Prisha hugged her tight.

'One last question,' she asked, 'is it okay to be a little despo when the guy simply won't take any step?'

'If you want him, you want him. Period.'

If I want him, I want him. Period. Prisha thought and grinned from ear to ear.

Within a week, Prisha moved in with Gauri and Diggy. She told Zinnia that she wanted to do group studies as the course was progressively becoming more and more rigorous. The same excuse was given to her parents. They were convinced once Prisha introduced them to Gauri and walked them through the flat on a video call. Diggy was intentionally kept out of the frame. As far as her parents were concerned, living with a boy was non-negotiable no matter how harmless he was.

There was a small garden behind the G-Punch office. It served as an unofficial smoking zone, which was frequented by Saveer. Prisha had been eyeing the spot for a long time. She bought a packet of Marlboro and feigned that she was a smoker too.

'Since when?' a colleague asked.

Prisha thought for a moment and said, 'Today.'

She went to the garden the moment she spotted Saveer. She smiled at him when he saw her. She had practiced a bit of smoking the night earlier with Gauri and Diggy. At the opportune moment, she feigned looking for her lighter which, of course, she had never carried.

'I have one,' Saveer said. Prisha immediately went up to him. She lit her smoke and took a puff.

'Never saw you here before,' he said.

'Just started recently,' she replied, smiling awkwardly.

'Not patronizing you but it isn't good,' Saveer said in a serious tone.

'Okay. And this is coming from someone who smokes daily.' Prisha looked amused.

How do I tell you that I deserve everything that's bad, Saveer wondered, and said, 'It's a habit. You have only just started.'

'Does that mean you take time letting go of things?' she asked.

Saveer took a long puff and thought about the question. Did he take time? No. He simply didn't let go off them. He exhaled and said, 'I don't.'

'And how fast do you open up to new things? Or . . .' Prisha smoked nervously and added, 'people?'

'I rarely welcome new people, a new routine or anything new in my life,' he said, dabbing the cigarette on the wall and throwing it into a dustbin.

'Excuse me.' He headed back to the office. Looking at his retreating figure, Prisha felt empty inside. *How long will I try? How long would he remain indifferent?*

'Saveer!' Prisha called him. He stopped and turned around.

'Remember you once told me about the saddest word you'd read: *almost?*'

He nodded slightly.

'I've found another, which is equally sad,' she said, joining him.

'*Supposed to.* I was *supposed to* be happy. I was *supposed to* be loved. He was *supposed to* be mine. I was *supposed to* be with him.'

Saveer kept looking at her as if he'd seen her for the first time.

'And the most unlucky ones are those who have experienced both *almost* and *supposed to.* I think I'm heading towards being one.' She flashed a sad smile at him. It was now his turn to watch her retreating figure.

Prisha didn't see Saveer anymore that day. It was evening by the time she finished work. Every day, the sense of fighting a losing battle surged within her. It was slowly turning her into an emotional wreck. Was she destined for another heartbreak? She kept asking herself and refused to listen to the answer.

She had asked her mother to courier her, her driving license from Faridabad. So she could now use Diggy's two-wheeler to ride between college, office and flat. When she went to where the two-wheeler was parked outside the office, she found there were cigarette stubs on the seat. She looked around and dusted off the stubs, before driving off. Since she had brushed away the stubs a little too hurriedly, she had missed two things. Firstly, the stubs looked like they had been broken meticulously and arranged into a word:

'STAY AWAY'.

Secondly, the cigarettes were of the same brand that Saveer smoked.

22

It was one of those days when he had to push himself in the gym. The inner pain wasn't enough. He had to inflict some outer pain to distract himself. But it wasn't working. He was on his fifth set of high-rep range, finding it impossible with every count. Once he was done, Saveer stepped out, sat down on one of the empty benches, at the corner of the gym and drank some water. Prisha had surprised him. And it had happened because he had taken her for granted. What more could an eighteen-year-old feel towards him other than infatuation? But what she had told him in office, hours ago, was something even he hadn't thought of earlier. *Supposed to . . .* With those words she had brought to light the other spectrum of his existence, which he hadn't thought about till then. Will a day come when he would tell himself the same: I was *supposed to* live. I was *supposed to* be happy. I was *supposed to* move on. Doesn't matter how much the weight of the past, should one make the present bear it? Saveer hadn't asked this to himself in five years. Why now? Was there something that was staring at him and he wasn't looking at it intentionally? When Isha had happened to him after his best friend had died, he took his time. But he did give it a chance. Was it time to give something else a chance? Someone else a chance?

Saveer went and skipped five hundred times, non-stop. He stretched a bit and then went to the shower. He realized he wanted to talk to someone. He missed sharing his thoughts with another person. What are thoughts? Footprints we follow to reach words. What are words? A bridge that connects us to others. He wanted to build a bridge to reach out to someone tonight. Saveer turned off the shower knob, wrapped a towel around his waist and came out. He pulled his phone out from his locker and called his assistant.

'Hello,' Krishna said.

'Hi, could you please send me Prisha Srivastav's number?'

'Certainly.'

Saveer saved her number. A gut feeling told him that he would need it more than he ever thought he would.

Prisha, Gauri and Diggy were in Sotally Tober pub. While Prisha was sitting on a couch, the other two were grooving to the music on the dance floor. They were celebrating their first salary. They'd pooled in Rs 5000 each and promised not to step out of the pub till all the money was spent. Prisha, however, wasn't drinking as much as she usually did. In fact, she was still sipping her first LIT when Diggy and Gauri had reached their third. Snatches of her conversation with Saveer in the garden earlier that day kept coming back to her. She understood that perhaps Saveer would never warm up to her. Whether it was due to her age, his ex-girlfriend, or something else, she didn't know. And even if she did, she knew it probably wouldn't change anything. And if that were the case, then she would resign from G-Punch soon. Otherwise, she would end up in an attractive loop of hopelessness, which Gauri had once mentioned. For a moment, she thought she could have done without another mess so soon after her last one. As she finished her drink, Prisha got a call from an unknown number.

'Hello? Hello?' She knew there was someone talking at the other end but the music was deafening. She cut the line. A True Caller pop-up flashed the name of the caller: S. Rathod. Prisha's eyes grew wide open. *This had better not be a fucking prank or coincidence else I'll kill the caller*, she thought and immediately stood up. Before Gauri and Diggy could notice, she slipped out of the pub. Then she called back. Saveer picked up the phone after the fourth ring.

'Hello,' he said. She didn't know how to thank him. She could have done anything for him at that instant.

'Hi!' She didn't care if her excitement was too obvious. This was their first phone call. And more than that this phone call was what happens when your team needs seven runs in one ball. It was not only a sixer but also a no ball. It blew away whatever impossibility Prisha had been pondering over a few minutes ago.

'Am I disturbing you?' Saveer asked.

'No, not at all. I was just in the . . . forget it. I wasn't doing anything. Please tell me.'

'I don't know how to beat about the bush. I wanted to talk.'

'Yeah sure. Let's talk.' Prisha wouldn't have been surprised if the whole city could hear her heartbeat at that moment.

'I want to meet and talk.'

Fuck, this phone call is a dream, she thought and said, 'Where do I meet you?'

'You don't have to. I will. Where are you?'

'I'm outside Sotally Tober, Koramangala.'

'I'll be there soon.' He cut the call.

Prisha went inside and dragged Gauri and Diggy down from the dance floor. She told them she was going out with Saveer.

'Going out? Are you sure it isn't an official meeting? After all he is our boss,' Diggy said.

'Shut up!' Prisha said and gulped down his drink. Diggy made a face. She alone wouldn't be able to handle him.

'LIT is a saviour,' she yelled over the music, excitement etched all over her face.

'All the best, bro,' Gauri said, heading back towards the dance floor.

It started drizzling as she stepped out of the pub. She prayed for Saveer to not cancel the plan. She was about to call him when she heard a car honking. One look and she knew the white Audi was his. It was on the opposite side of the road. She dashed towards the car, trying not to get drenched in the rain. As she got inside and strapped on the seat belt, the car vroomed past the pub.

They were on Nice Road. True to its name, it was an empty stretch, with no vehicles ahead or behind them. Every once in a while, a car whooshed past. The drizzle outside, the lonely road, the dark night and the fact that they were inches away from each other was too good to be true for Prisha. She was sure it was a dream. 'I'm sorry for this abrupt plan,' Saveer said.

'I'm not complaining. But what made you meet me . . . like this?' Prisha asked softly. She didn't know whether it was the AC or his presence that gave her goosebumps. He understood and raised the temperature.

'Thanks,' she murmured.

'Let's talk straight, Prisha.'

The way he took her name . . . she sighed. There was always an intense air around him, which was both sexually and emotionally arresting.

'What is it?' she asked.

'That's my question. What is it? Your friend told me you had a crush on me but every time we talk, even if it is an office matter, there is more in your eyes than there should be.'

He noticed my eyes, the way I noticed his, Prisha thought. 'Gauri told you that?'

'She did. But let's not change the topic.'

'I think I answered you long ago when you were at my place. Remember?'

Saveer remembered the night but not her answer.

'I want to know you,' Prisha said.

'Knowing takes time.'

'Then I want to spend time with you.' She was quick.

'Spending time will need a lifetime's investment.'

'I want to.'

'What if I tell you I didn't bluff about killing my girlfriend? That I'm indeed dangerous.'

Prisha thought for some time. She would one day know exactly what he meant when he said he killed his girlfriend. He could not mean it literally. But for now, there was something else which she should tell him.

'What if . . .' Prisha glanced at him once and then straight ahead of her at the dark road, 'I tell you I'm in love with you.'

Prisha felt Saveer accelerating the car.

'What if I tell you your words have haunted me? When you said I helped you unlearn your past. And today when you said you are heading towards experiencing both the *almost* and the *supposed to* aspects of your life.'

'May I know why exactly they haunted you? Since they were both about me and not about you.'

'So you think. What I helped you gain, I couldn't do it myself.'

'Did you try hard enough?'

'Not until now. Not until . . .'

It was the first time he had not finished what he had started. 'Not until . . . ?'

'Not until we met.'

Prisha knew she could cry at any moment. She wasn't ready to show him her vulnerability. She was someone who preferred crying alone.

'As you said, let's not beat about the bush. I'll ask you straight: do you want to . . .' Prisha began.

'Don't say any further,' Saveer said and took a turn. Neither talked till he stopped the car in front of the lane where her apartment was. Prisha climbed out. The drizzle had stopped by then. She was confused. The thrill of the drive seemed to have dissipated. As if it was nothing. She preferred to remain quiet as she pushed open the apartment gate.

'Prisha,' Saveer said. She turned and noticed he was already out of the car. He walked up to her and hugged her tight—his first in five years.

'When you say everything, it kills the magic,' he whispered into her ears. He broke apart from her and without waiting for her to respond, got into the car and drove off.

Saveer felt sleepy during dinner and left midway to sleep early. He didn't know his dinner was spiked. Next morning, while taking a shower, he didn't notice a small 'I' tattooed on his back.

23

By the time Gauri and Diggy came back home, they found Prisha asleep. They were eager to know what had happened but finding her asleep, they too called it a night. Prisha was awake the whole time, smiling to herself. The hug and Saveer's parting words tickled her senses through the night. For the first time in a long time, she got up feeling fresh even though she hadn't slept a wink.

It was while going to college in a cab that she shared the details with Gauri.

'So it began with a tight hug,' Gauri repeated.

'It wasn't all that tight,' Prisha lied. She could still feel his chest.

'I'm sure the next one will be.'

Prisha blushed. She didn't remember the last time she had blushed like this. She had saved his number but found he wasn't on WhatsApp. She had texted him a 'Good Morning' but there wasn't a response. She was itching to call him but somehow managed to control that urge.

'He hugged you. You messaged him. So now it is his turn to contact you,' Gauri said.

'Are you sure?'

'In the beginning it is better to follow these simple unsaid rules.'

Which I never did with Utkarsh, Prisha thought. 'Okay, I won't call him.'

From morning till lunchtime, there was neither any message nor any call. Prisha kept snatching Gauri's and Diggy's phones to call herself and check if the connectivity was all right.

'Should I go to office?' she asked.

'I don't think so. Not today at least,' said Diggy.

'Diggy is right. Not today.'

'I haven't felt this impatient ever in my life,' Prisha said hiding her face in her hands.

'Chill. Call him tomorrow,' Gauri advised.

When they walked out of college in the evening, Prisha froze at the sight right opposite her college gates. She nudged Gauri. 'Just look right ahead of you. Do not make it obvious but is it real?'

'OMG! Now that was completely unpredictable!' Gauri exclaimed.

'Isn't that . . . ?' Diggy began.

'Diggy, let's leave,' Gauri cut him short and dragged him away, showing a thumbs-up to Prisha.

She was suddenly nervous seeing Saveer standing against his car outside her college. She took a few deep breaths and started walking towards him slowly. He waved at her. He wasn't smiling. She waved back, smiling.

'Hi. What are you doing here?' she asked.

'Is that even a question?' Saveer said.

'Okay, I wasn't expecting you here.'

'Trust me, even I did not expect myself to be here.' He then gestured towards the car. 'Shall we?'

'Can we please take a selfie?'

Saveer knew what a selfie was. But it wasn't a rage five years ago. He didn't remember if he had ever taken one with Isha. Now, standing next to Prisha, he didn't know how to pose. As they stood close to each other, she was a tad uncomfortable as well. He could smell the fragrance of her hair and she could smell Pour Homme on him. Prisha held up her phone. The moment the front camera clicked, Saveer truly saw himself for the first time in five years. He was pulled back in time. However, he didn't look anything like he used to with Isha.

'It would be better if you click,' Prisha said and gave her phone to him. He held the phone up and finally clicked. He checked the photograph.

'Why are you looking so polished?' he asked.

'It's an app filter. Don't you use it?'

'I rarely click myself,' he said. Then they got into the car and drove off.

'You asked what was I doing here? I received your message in the morning and was sceptical about the reply. I thought about it the entire day. And I arrived at a conclusion.'

'What conclusion?'

'That I have become that person who can't think and be in any relationship anymore. I should find myself in the middle of one to appreciate it, to take care of it and most importantly, with no options to ignore it. Only then will I be able to have a relationship.'

'And coming to pick me up from college makes you feel . . .'

'That I'm already in a . . .'

Prisha grabbed his hand, which was on top of the gear.

'Don't say it. Someone recently told me saying everything kills the magic,' she said. Saveer looked at her and smiled. His first smile at her. Prisha understood it was the beginning.

If we consider the world as one giant mind, then Saveer and Prisha were separate stories, living in different corners of that mind. But at that moment, when he smiled at her, they dissolved into one another to form a single story. For Prisha, he wasn't a blank canvas to be filled in with colours. He already had colours, layers of it, and she had to understand their composition. He was closed, and to open him up was what Prisha looked forward to expectantly. She couldn't believe it when she learnt that Saveer didn't have any friends or family. Not even a single person. His office people knew him, he knew them. And that was the only social interaction he would have. Mean Monster never met a girl twice. Prisha was happy now he that he had her. Only her.

She would never let him stay alone on weekends. They would meet somewhere quiet and talk or scout good places to eat. Prisha consciously avoided bringing up Isha. They went for movies and every time there was an opportunity for an intimate gesture, she would wait for him to take charge. But he never did. In the months that followed, Prisha couldn't think of a single moment when he tried to touch her. If she held his hand during a movie, he would change his position. If she held his hand while traipsing in a mall or on a lonely road, he would squirm and get uncomfortable. She never mentioned it to him, but discussed it with Gauri.

'Maybe he needs time,' Gauri said.

'If it is a matter of time then it is okay but . . .'

'You think he doesn't take the lead because you are too young for him?'

'That could be a reason as well, right?'

'Well, depends.'

'Depends on?'

'If he is used to 36D, then 32B would make him uncomfortable.'

'Shut up! Please tell me you are kidding.'

'I am, of course! I don't think he is into you for sexual needs like Sanjeev. His love for you isn't false. That's what I feel.'

His love isn't false . . . that was music to Prisha's ears.

'I'll wait. Patience is the key I guess.'

'It always is,' Gauri said.

For Saveer, Prisha was like a warm summer breeze in an Arctic climate. He was still adjusting to it. Saveer was happy at the pace at which their relationship was progressing. Had they kept on hesitating, this day would have never arrived.

Prisha was a bit immature, Saveer was aware of it. However, he found her childlike innocence and impulsiveness endearing. She was everything that Saveer wasn't. There were times when she would keep on talking and he would want to make insane love to her. But he held himself back, not wanting to do anything until he was sure. He understood what she wanted when she held his hand in the movie hall or on a road. He kept asking himself if he was ready. They would meet more and more often and talk at length, but being the older one, certain questions kept popping up in his mind.

A thirty-four-year-old man and an eighteen-year-old can surely fall in love but what if they decide to take it to the next level, in which society gets involved? Is it feasible?

What if he invests himself in this relationship but his past catches up to him, like it had with Isha?

The only thing Saveer was confident of was that Prisha would be the last girl he would involve himself with. And he would make sure nothing went wrong. Come what may.

And then there was the most important question: What if he ended up killing Prisha, like he had killed Isha, his best friend, his school crush, his dog, his mother, his father, his uncle and his brother?

24

It was Friday evening when he accepted Prisha's invitation for dinner to her flat. She was over the moon. With Gauri's assistance, she decided the menu and the drinks and selected her dress. An hour before Saveer was about to arrive, Diggy and Gauri left.

'Call us when it is over,' Gauri said and winked. Diggy hugged her, saying, 'You are the torchbearer for all eighteen-year-olds who are considered kids. Just show it to him you aren't one.'

'Shut up and get lost. You guys are making me nervous,' Prisha laughed and closed the door. She checked herself in the mirror. She had put on a little bit of make-up—lipstick, eyeliner and a little blusher. She didn't want to look gaudy on a dinner date at home. But no less desirable either. In fact, while fixing her hair, Gauri had told her about the plan.

'It happens in the movies that way. First, you invite the person, then you dress up for him; he will get you a gift and will also be well-dressed. You two will enjoy a good conversation, have dinner—make sure the lighting is dim.

It will create an ambience and before the person leaves, there's bound to be a return gift.' The last part hinted at a naughty twist. It made Prisha both nervous and excited. It also made her buy a white satin negligee in anticipation. She had a plan. It was high time he showed her why the so-called *other women*, who had never mattered to him, had given him the title of the Mean Monster. Until then, he had shown no signs of being one.

Saveer reached at five minutes to eight. He looked dapper in a blue Zara jacket and black trousers. He had a bouquet of fresh red roses—her favourite—and a huge packet of multi-flavoured macarons. She wanted to kiss him on the cheek but settled for a tight hug.

'Where are Gauri and Diggy?' Saveer asked, stepping in.

'They have some work,' she said. They looked at each other and laughed out loud.

'Sorry, I didn't want them to be here tonight.'

'I understand.'

You do? She thought. Looking at the macarons, she said, 'May I have them? I can't help myself.'

She was having problem sequencing everything in her mind because somewhere she was anticipating the post-dinner part, maybe a little too much.

'Sure,' he smiled.

She had one and offered another to Saveer. They looked at each other as they munched on the macarons.

'Can I ask you something?' Prisha asked.

'Yeah.'

'What do you think of me?' She noticed his eyebrows twitch a little as if he wasn't expecting the question. Her gaze remained steadfastly on him. He took his time to respond.

'Only when you will understand it without my telling you so in words, I shall conclude that it's because I really felt it from my heart.'

She could have kissed him to death at that moment.

'That's the best part about you,' she said. 'You talk as if you are some audiobook written by some author.'

Saveer smiled, saying, 'Life's shit makes you more articulate.'

'You've seen a lot, isn't it?'

Saveer nodded. Prisha was tempted to ask about Isha and what exactly he'd meant when he'd said he'd killed her.

'Is Isha a part of the lot that you have seen?' Prisha was careful how she phrased it. She knew it was a sensitive issue for him.

'Can we please not talk about it?' Saveer said.

'Does that mean you still love her?' Prisha said and regretted saying so immediately.

'This phrase—still love her—makes me feel like love has an expiry date. All I know is Isha is a part of my system now. Even if I try, I would not be able to *not love her*. She has been tattooed into my soul.'

Tattooed into his soul . . . Prisha's lips had parted by the time he had finished. She promised herself to fight the world to have him by her side and to hold on to him for dear life. She recalled arguing with her friends in Faridabad over the existence of true love. She'd usually win such arguments but after Utkarsh broke her heart, she realized how meaningless those victories were. And then she met Saveer.

'You all right?' Saveer sounded concerned. Prisha realized her eyes were moist.

'Excuse me,' she said and headed to the washroom. She took a few deep breaths to control her tears, lest the kohl got smudged. After she got a grip on herself, she went back to Saveer and made sure the conversation remained light for the rest of the dinner.

'When do you go shopping?' she asked, looking at his jacket.

'Online. I rarely go out.'

'You mean you *used to* rarely go out.' Her emphasis on the two words amused Saveer. He knew what she meant.

'Yeah, used to. Someone's pulling me out all the time these days.'

'Is that a complaint?'

'Does it sound like one?'

They talked, dined, drank and talked some more. In between, she kept updating Gauri on the phone. That was the deal, else Gauri threatened to barge in on them.

We are almost done with the food and drinks, Prisha texted.

Brace yourself girl. The moment is coming, Gauri responded. *Damn, I'm already getting goosebumps.*

Are you wet?

Shut up!

Once they were done with dinner, Prisha took him to her bedroom.

'Okay, I've got something for you,' she said.

'Yeah?'

'It's a little something. Just close your eyes for a few seconds.'

'Seriously?'

'Yeah. Please. I'm not going to harm you,' she said in mock seriousness.

'All right,' Saveer said and closed his eyes. A few seconds went by. He heard a sound and then Prisha said, 'Okay, open your eyes now.'

All that Saveer could see was Prisha standing in front of the bedroom door. He shrugged.

'Give me a second,' Prisha moved behind the door and shut it. It was then that he noticed a poster on the door, which she had pasted while his eyes were closed. It had a cute puppy on it and a line in Hindi that read:

Main badi kutti cheez hun (I'm a bitchy thing).

Saveer couldn't help but laugh out.

'I mean it,' Prisha said.

'If you mean it, I believe it,' Saveer laughed, 'but where did you go?'

The door was pushed open.

'In here.' Prisha appeared in a white satin negligee. Saveer stopped laughing. He knew where they were heading next. She switched off the tube light and switched on a bulb, bathing the room in a dim red light. Then she came close to him. He was sitting on the floor, next to the mattress. She pulled him up. Suddenly, there was pin-drop silence in the house. Prisha stood on her toes to kiss Saveer. Her eyes were closed and she was expecting him to undress her. Instead, he placed his hand on her shoulders and said, 'We need to give it some more time.'

Prisha opened her eyes. She wanted to know why but stopped as he leaned close to her and whispered in her ear.

'One more thing. Skin can only claim, but only a soul can win a soul.' He smiled at her, caressed her cheeks and then left.

Prisha stood there. With that one line he had stripped her bare. And no clothes would ever cover her up in front of him again. She heard a bike roar downstairs. She ran to the window, parted the curtains and looked down. Saveer was already looking towards her window. She waved at him. He didn't. *Did I upset him?* He drove off.

Prisha was about to draw the curtains when she noticed a woman standing next to the gate of her apartment. The woman was looking up at her. In the faint glow of the streetlight, Prisha could only see her silhouette, her face was hidden in darkness.

'What do you want?' Prisha asked. There was no answer. The woman didn't move.

'I'm talking to you,' Prisha yelled.

The woman turned and walked out of the lane.

'Weird,' Prisha muttered and drew the curtains.

25

H e didn't even kiss you?' Gauri asked.

'No.' Prisha sounded a bit lost. They had come to
buy groceries from the departmental store next to their
apartment in the morning. Prisha had intentionally
avoided talking about last night with her flatmates. She
was too spellbound to care for a discussion.

'The first time Sanjeev was here, he was all over me,'
Gauri said, picking up a basket.

'That's precisely why I'm so stuck up on Saveer.
He is not your ordinary testosterone man,' Prisha
said. She went towards the noodles section, followed
by Gauri. She placed a few packets of noodles in the
basket.

'Well, I know what you mean,' Gauri said, agreeing.

'He told me that skin can only claim but a soul can
win another soul. I mean I can't tell you how lucky I felt
at that moment. And I realized if a man does something
unexpected of his sex in a particular situation, then you
can count on him. What say?' Prisha picked up a bottle of

ketchup and placed it in the basket. She looked at Gauri and realized that she was staring at her.

'What?' Prisha shrugged.

'You are making me jealous now.'

Prisha laughed and then said, 'Sorry, I didn't mean to.'

'Of course you did. You are a bitch. I know that.'

'Shut up! And tell me what should I do?' They headed towards the sanitary napkin corner.

'What should you do? You have a rare guy in love with you and you are asking me what you should do? Are you stupid? Just marry him.'

Prisha blushed. 'I wish that happens. But what I meant was I think I upset him last night. I tried calling him in the morning but he didn't pick up. It won't end because of last night's silliness, right?'

Gauri looked amused. She picked up a packet of Whisper. 'Saveer always came across as a mature man. If it ends because of this, then he will have to be the greatest BC on earth.'

'I don't want your opinion. Give me your suggestions. What should I do?'

'Are you going to office today?'

'I am.'

'Ask him directly if he is upset. It's better to straighten things out at times.'

'Hmm.'

The two shuffled towards the snacks section.

Prisha went to office post lunch, after attending an important class. She was hoping to bump into Saveer during a coffee or smoke break, but she didn't. He came out of the cabin just once to talk to an accounts department employee. When she tried to catch his eye, he deliberately didn't look at her.

'Ignoring me?' Prisha felt offended. *You aren't allowed to ignore me, mister*, she thought. She went to the office pantry. There was nobody there. She picked up a knife. Then she went to the parking lot and punctured one of the tyres of Saveer's car. She smiled, satisfied. Now he would have to ask someone to drop him home. Enter, Prisha . . . the drum rolls had hardly begun in the corridors of her mind when she looked up and noticed a CCTV camera right on top of her. It was a face-palm moment for her. Her happiness deflated like the punctured tyre. She went inside feeling like a loser.

Prisha finished her work quickly, hoping to leave before her mischief was caught. She started the scooty and was about to drive off when Saveer called her— further embarrassment looming in the horizon.

'Hi,' she said.

'Going home?' he asked.

'Yeah.'

'Actually, someone punctured one of my tyres,' he said, joining her.

Prisha gulped anxiously.

'Oh really?' she said in a small voice, wishing to dig a hole and disappear into it at that moment.

'Not really someone. It's a girl,' he went on.

Prisha wanted to close her eyes and pretend that she didn't exist.

'To be honest, it's a girl I happen to be in love with,' Saveer smiled mischievously.

Prisha went beetroot red.

'I'm so sorry. You were ignoring me and I . . .' she apologized.

'You had better be sorry. And your punishment is you have to drop me home,' he said.

'Yes, sir.'

He climbed on to the pillion seat.

'Let's go.'

As they rode off, he placed his hands on her waist. She didn't know if it was intentional but she felt like riding forever. Every time the scooty ran over a pothole or hit a bumper, she swerved it in such a way that their bodies touched. It gave her a wicked satisfaction. Though he was talking to her every now and then, she kept responding in monosyllables. She concentrated more on this unintentional intimacy than on his intentional words.

'Any other service, sir?' she asked as they reached his house.

'You always asked what I did when I'm at home.'

Prisha nodded.

'Why don't you come in and have a look?'

For a moment, they stared at each other. 'Okay,' she finally said, licking her lips. Prisha had never confessed it but to see him in his private space, when nobody was around, had been a fantasy of hers. Just to watch him go about his normal chores would be a sexual and a romantic high.

As she entered his house, the first thing that struck Prisha was how cavernous it was.

'Don't you think this place is a little too big for one person?' she asked, making herself comfortable on the couch.

Saveer sat opposite her and said, 'I don't live here alone.'

'Who else do you stay with?' Prisha was curious.

'Isha wanted to stay in a duplex. And I live here with her memories. When you live somewhere with someone's memories, no place is big enough. Trust me.'

Prisha felt vaguely threatened for the first time in her relationship. What was worse was that she couldn't identify the source of the threat. Her initial excitement dimmed a little.

'Let me get you some water,' Saveer said, getting up.

'You go ahead and change. I'll fetch it myself.' It was Prisha's defence reaction towards the just-realized threat, which was yet to be decoded. She was in a relationship with this man. She shouldn't act formal or uncomfortable in a place he called home.

'Which way is the kitchen?' she asked, standing up as well. Saveer showed her the way and went upstairs. She loved the way the rooms lit up every time Saveer stepped into one. 'I love the lighting,' she remarked.

'Isha's idea,' Saveer smiled and disappeared into his bedroom.

Prisha could now put a name to the threat. She went to the kitchen and opened a huge refrigerator. There were beer cans, milk, eggs, cottage cheese and some vegetables. She picked up one of the water bottles and finished half of it. Then she got out of the kitchen. She walked around the house, taking in the tasteful decoration—the false ceiling, the lamps, the thick curtains. Finally, she reached the flight of stairs leading up to the bedroom. She decided to go up on the first floor. As she placed her foot on the first step, the staircase lit up, illuminating Isha and Saveer's photographs on the adjacent wall. Finally, Prisha could put a face to the name. She took down every photograph and inspected each minutely, trying to understand Saveer and Isha's relationship through them.

Isha was not drop-dead gorgeous but as Prisha realized, there was something about her, which made one look at her a little longer than necessary. She could judge the kind of intimacy Saveer had shared with her from the pictures. And it disturbed her. Would she ever be able to achieve that kind of intimacy with him? It wasn't just sexual intimacy but a spiritual connection as well—something sacred. A relationship devoid of any insecurity, too pure to be tainted by societal judgements and simply unbreakable.

And after all this he had killed her? He must be joking, Prisha took a deep sigh. *I'll know soon.*

'Come up,' Saveer called her. She hung the frame in her hand back on the wall and went up, followed by darkness.

Saveer had changed into a T-shirt and a pair of trousers. The kind of boyish charm he exuded made Prisha think he didn't look a day older than twenty-six.

'Did you feel bad about yesterday? If so, then I'm sorry,' Prisha said, sitting on the couch opposite the bed.

Saveer looked at her. His gaze burnt a hole in her and she was left to look for an answer in its ashes.

'I don't want to scar you, Prisha,' he said.

'What do you mean?'

'I mean you are my last. I don't want to take any chances with you.'

'And you are my only. If I take chances, it had better be with you,' she said. There was silence. She could sense his breath quickening. So did hers.

'The fire that can provide you warmth can also burn you if you go too close to it,' he said.

'Do me a favour, Saveer. Just burn me.' As she said those words, he stood up and came around to where she was sitting. He cupped her face in his hands and sucked her lower lip harder than usual. She shut her eyes, her face contorted, reacting to the pain. He wasn't giving her a chance to respond to the kiss. It was just him, sucking her lips, her tongue. The way he was holding her face made her feel controlled. Submission was never this sexy, she thought. And in no time, there was a rhythm to the kissing and all she could do was groove to it. She felt ecstatic. The spell soon broke as a car started honking outside.

'Guess it is not time yet,' he said jocularly, trying to negate the awkwardness that the honking had set in.

Saveer went to the window, parted the curtains and yelled, 'What the fuck!' Prisha joined him. They rushed downstairs. He opened the main door. His car was parked outside the house. And it was his car's horn that had gone off on its own.

26

Saveer dashed towards his car. He tried opening the door but it was locked. It unlocked after a moment. He turned around. Prisha was standing on the steps holding the keys.

'They were on the doorstep,' she said. Inside the car, someone had stuck a chewing gum on the horn. He removed it and the honking stopped. People in nearby houses were peeping out from their windows and terraces to see what the racket was all about. They went inside.

'Was this a prank?' Prisha asked. Saveer was thoughtful. He noticed the punctured tyre had been replaced.

'Let me call Krishna.' Saveer went back inside. Prisha followed him. Saveer looked for his phone in the hall first and then in the bedroom.

'I think I've misplaced it,' he said.

'Should I call Krishna? I too have his number,' Prisha offered. Saveer nodded. She called and gave the phone to him.

'Hi, Krishna, this is Saveer here.'

'Hi, sir.'

'Do you have any idea who got my car from office?'

'I did.'

'You did?'

'Yes, you had texted me saying that I had to fix the tyre and park the car outside your house and place the keys on the doorstep,' Krishna said. Saveer knew he always did as instructed. The question was who had instructed him.

'Did you say I texted you?'

'Yes. I still have the text.'

'Could you tell me the time of the text?'

'Sure sir,' Krishna said and added a few seconds later, '6.30 p.m.'

That's roughly around the same time Prisha gave me the lift from office. Did I lose my phone then? Saveer wondered but he couldn't be sure. He thanked Krishna and cut the line. He was ready to go to the police station and file a complaint about the missing phone when Prisha surprised him by saying, 'Here's your phone.'

Saveer frowned and took it.

'Where did you get it?'

'I called your number from the landline when you were talking to Krishna. Then I heard it ringing somewhere close. It was on the doorstep as well. We hadn't noticed it before.'

'That's weird. Who would text Krishna on my behalf?'

'By any chance, did you forget about it?'

'Forget about what? The text or the fact that I lost my phone? Or that I had kept it on the doorstep? I'm not that old.' He sounded somewhat frustrated.

'I know. I'm sorry, I just . . .'

'It's okay. It has to be a prank. Why else would someone paste the chewing gum on the horn?'

Right when we were having a special moment, Prisha thought.

'Probably it was my mistake. Maybe I dropped the phone while climbing on the scooty. Someone must have noticed it,' Saveer said. He thought for a while and then added, 'I think I should drop you home.' Prisha was disappointed. Everything was going smoothly till someone played the stupid prank.

Saveer dropped Prisha home on his bike.

As she lay on her bed, Prisha tried to recall the kiss, but couldn't revel in its afterglow as Isha's face kept coming back to her. She thought about their relationship. Isha lived within Saveer and as long as he housed her in his heart, how could she ever enter it? Saveer had uprooted Utkarsh from her heart, mind, body and soul, but had she been able to erase Isha's traces from him? If Saveer hadn't yet let go of Isha, would he ever be able to love Prisha with all his heart? Or would she always play second fiddle to Isha? Such thoughts tormented Prisha.

I'm with Prisha because I can't be with Isha?

She remembered the discussion she had once had with Saveer. She now understood conclusively that break-ups were easier than losing a loved one.

From that day onwards, every time they met, Prisha made sure they clicked loads of photographs. She was making a collection. Once it reached 100, she printed them out, bought flimsy frames and gifted them to him. He asked her to choose where the frames should be put up. Prisha wanted to tell Saveer to remove the ones he had with Isha but she couldn't. She put them up all over the house and even above Saveer and Isha's photographs. It gave her a weird kind of satisfaction. She knew she could not do anything to sever Isha's memories from Saveer so she derived vicarious pleasure by doing this.

Prisha was expecting a reaction when Saveer saw their photographs above Isha's and his but he only smiled at her. Looking at himself in the photographs, with Isha and Prisha, he distinguished a difference in the way he used to smile back then and now. *Just like there was a difference between the silence preceding and succeeding a storm, our smiles too changed before and after a life-storm.*

'You know,' Prisha said, 'I think you smile slightly differently now.'

And the one who noticed the difference was the one who would add to the smile with time, Saveer thought. He hugged her gently.

In every relationship, people fall into a routine over time. On weekdays, Saveer and Prisha would see each other in office and on weekends, she would go over to his place. It was a weekend-live-in set up. Prisha cooked for him, read to him when he shaved, watched him shower, cuddled with him at night. Days were spent sipping red wine and lying on the terrace together at night.

One night while they were lying on the terrace, she requested him to change his ringtone. Saveer was taken by surprise.

'It confuses me,' she said. *It stabs me*, she meant. Saveer looked at her for a long time and then gave her the phone. 'You choose.'

She had never thought it would be that easy. Prisha immediately changed the ringtone to Enrique's Wanna *Be With You*. Then she held him and smiled. Just then, his phone rang. It was a business call. As he took it, he turned his back to her. Prisha noticed a small tattoo on his back, right below his shoulder. She looked closely at it. It looked like an 'I'. *I for. . . Isha.* Her smile faded. He ended the call and turned around to face her.

'I have to leave. I've to finish loads of assignments,' she said abruptly.

'Should I drop you back?'

Prisha shook her head and gave him a peck on the cheek. 'I'll manage.' She left.

What does one do about thorns, which poke from time to time, on a rosy bed of a relationship? Do you ignore them or do you uproot them? Or do you take it up with your partner?

Prisha didn't know why Saveer had never made love to her. It wasn't as if she had sex on her mind all the time but it was natural for two people in a relationship to communicate through their bodies. On the one hand, he had destroyed the SIM that he had used to hook up with women as the Mean Monster and on the other, the maximum physical intimacy she had shared with him were a tight hug and a peck. She was hoping that the kiss would have been a prelude to further intimacy but nothing happened. What was he waiting for? Or scared of?

'Did you guys make love?' Prisha asked one Sunday afternoon, while she was watering his plants on the terrace. Saveer was planting a few more in another corner. He paused after hearing the question and then resumed his work, asking, 'Who?'

'Isha and you?'

'We did.'

'Weren't you afraid of scaring her as well?' Prisha asked. She was carefully watering the plants. The last two words told Saveer what Prisha really wanted to know. *I wasn't afraid of scaring her. I was afraid of killing her. Still, I took a chance. And now she is gone.* Saveer had realized his mistake of not telling Isha the truth. And he was repeating the same mistake with Prisha as well. In both the cases, one thing was common: his dogged desire to not lose the loves of his life.

'There is a time for everything,' he said. She was happy to know that he understood what she had wanted to tell him. However, she never understood why time was so important to him when she was already his. Was it because he hadn't been able to make up his mind if he was hers completely?

While lying on his bed that night, Saveer's mind wanted to come to a decision even as his heart was playing devil's advocate. What if he ended up killing Prisha as well? Isha was older but Prisha was still a teenager. He had to think twice before doing anything. Should he make the plunge? He closed his eyes, trying to think clearly but dozed off earlier than he thought he would. That night too his dinner was spiked. The next morning he again missed the fresh tiny tattoo on his back, right below the *I*. Together the two words now read: *I will*.

27

Time flew. While Prisha lamented over the fact that they weren't close enough on his birthday, Saveer was happy that they had come together after his thirty-fourth birthday. Prisha had planned to celebrate New Year's Eve with Saveer but her college closed for winter holidays and she had to go back home. At home in Faridabad, Saveer and Prisha stayed in touch with each other over regular video calls. However, Prisha realized that no matter how much they stayed electronically together, Saveer's absence only made her heart grow fonder and she pined for him. As soon as the holidays got over, she flew back to Bengaluru.

Prisha had worried that age might be deterring factor in their relationship, but over time, she realized that when two people fall in love, age doesn't matter. One might fall in love with someone of the same age, but if they didn't bond with him, then they would be on two different emotional islands, never feeling encouraged enough to bridge the gap. Prisha felt that she shared the same emotional ground with Saveer. She felt treasured by him.

Saveer was protective of her. And it aroused her. He was possessive but not controlling. The only thing that bothered Prisha was that he had never made any advances towards her even though he had the license to long ago. There were times she craved for intimacy, but didn't tell him. It wasn't the only thing she was with him for after all, she coaxed herself.

The weekend following her exams was Prisha's birthday. Although she had once mentioned it to him, she was doubtful if Saveer would remember.

At midnight, Prisha waited desperately for Saveer's call. Her parents and her sister had already wished her. Gauri and Diggy had bought a fruitcake, most of which they smeared on her face. They even had a mini party— beer, music and dancing. Prisha, however, was distracted. There had been no calls or messages from Saveer so far.

In the morning, Gauri and Diggy went to college to attend an important class, after which they promised to be with Prisha. They also planned to visit the office to check on Saveer. They too had noticed that he hadn't called her. Prisha woke up late, hearing the doorbell ring. She opened the door to find Krishna, Saveer's assistant. He was carrying a huge bouquet of roses. She took it from him, feeling excited.

'Sir asked me to give this to you.' He gave her an envelope as well.

'Where is he?' she asked.

'I'm not sure. He told me he won't be working today.'

'Okay. Thank you for this,' she said and closed the door behind her. She tore open the envelope. There was a note inside that read: *Happy birthday, Prisha. There is a ticket*. It was a flight ticket to Mumbai. She continued reading: *Fly down to Mumbai. A driver will be waiting for you outside the airport. He will bring you to me. Finally, the time has come. I'm waiting*.

She knew what he was talking about. She had four hours left. Prisha quickly got ready, texted Gauri that she was leaving for Mumbai and took a cab to the airport.

She felt restless throughout the journey. It was her first visit to Mumbai. The flight landed early in the evening. It didn't take her much time to spot the driver—he was holding a card bearing her name. She tried calling Saveer but his phone was unreachable. By the time the driver drove her to Gateway of India, it was already around eight in the evening.

Prisha had seen the Gateway of India only in pictures. She started looking around desperately for Saveer. His phone was still unreachable. As a flock of pigeons suddenly took flight, she spotted Saveer. She ran and hugged him.

'Happy birthday, sweetheart,' he whispered into her ears.

'Thank you.' She broke the hug and looked at him.

'Let's go,' he said.

'Where?'

'Do you trust me?'

'Even if you take me to the middle of the sea and leave me there, I still won't ask why.'

'Well, I'm doing exactly that.'

'Huh?'

Saveer scooped her up in his lap.

'And I thought I'm the one who is nineteen' she said, feeling blessed.

Saveer took Prisha to a yacht docked closed to the Gateway of India. Saveer had taken permission to sail at night. Soon, the city was a ring of golden light in the distant horizon.

Prisha cut a cake and Saveer uncorked a bottle of champagne and finished the two over light conversation.

It grew progressively chilly as they sailed further away from the city. The sea was calm, the night sky above was embellished with stars. And then, there they were, lying next to each other, looking up at the sky. A moment later, Saveer said, '*Naanu endendigu ninnavalagirabeku.*'

'What's that?'

'Something Isha would say a lot. It's in Kannada. It means I want to be yours forever.'

'Remember what you had told me about forever when we saw each other for the first time?' Prisha asked.

'Thanks for challenging that notion.'

They smiled at each other.

'This has been my best birthday so far,' she said softly.

'Don't jump to a conclusion so fast.'

She looked at him. He sat up.

'Are you ready for the Mean Monster, Prisha?' Saveer's eyes bore into hers.

Prisha took a deep breath and nodded. He pulled her up. Then he came closer.

Prisha was wearing a blue dress, with buttons in the front. He slowly tore it open. The buttons, one by one, fell on the yacht's floor. Prisha's lower lip started to tremble. His eyes were fixed on her. Prisha couldn't look at him. She blinked and looked elsewhere. He immediately cupped her face and said, 'You won't look away. I want you to witness everything.'

Prisha licked her lips and nodded. Her torso was bare except for her royal blue bra. She touched his chest gingerly. It had a fine sprinkling of hair and protruding nipples. He pulled down the rest of her dress. She was wearing a matching panty. Goosebumps dotted her skin. He looked her over. She had never found shyness more arousing. Saveer picked up her right hand and started sucking her fingers one at a time. He then kissed all the way up her arm till her shoulder. Then he licked his way to her earlobe. He held her hand.

Prisha squirmed as she felt tickled by his tongue. He released his hand and caressed her back, travelling all the way down to her panty. He put it inside and squeezed her butt hard. Her lips parted in shock. She immediately hid her face in his chest.

'I'm feeling shy, Saveer,' she said, covering her breasts and the erect nipples against his chest. He held her hands and stepped back, then he spread them and pushed them over her head.

'Open your eyes,' he said. She did and saw her right nipple inside his mouth. The pleasure of the sight was unprecedented. He sucked it. She wriggled her hand out of his grip and touched his groin. She unbuckled his belt, unzipped his jeans and then tugged it down along with his underwear. She felt his taut butt and whispered, 'I love this booty.'

He smirked, feeling her squeeze his butt.

'And what do you think about this?' Saveer said, placing her left hand on the shaft of his penis. Prisha was pleasantly shocked by the width of his organ. When she parted her lips, he was quick to shut them with his own, letting his tongue explore her mouth, while pulling down her panty.

Prisha felt his hand on her butt as he lifted her up— she wound her legs around his waist—and took her to a corner of the yacht while kissing her. He made her sit on the aluminium parapet. She could hear the waves lapping the side of the yacht. And sense the height of his passion in the way he touched her and kissed her.

'Hold on to me,' he whispered sexily.

Before she could put her arms around him, he slid down and held her by her waist. She gripped his hair tight as she felt his warm tongue brush against her vagina. He licked her hungrily. In no time, she felt like flying. Prisha moaned, at first softly and then loudly. She no longer felt strapped on to her body. The gates had been opened, she was free to leave, to fly, to wander, to conquer. Prisha moaned loudly as Saveer tongue-fucked a certain deep spot inside her. She knew she could come any time. And just when she thought she would, Saveer withdrew his tongue. It was as if she was free falling and just when she thought she'd hit the ground, someone scooped her up. Her heart was in her mouth.

Saveer picked her up in his arms and slowly placed her on the slightly wet yacht floor. The more she looked into his eyes, the more she told herself it was a spell. It wasn't real. Nothing real could be this beautiful. He kissed her forehead and then started going down on her slowly. When his lips reached her navel, he realized Prisha had stiffened a bit. He looked up at her. She was watching him. He smirked at her and spread her legs. The strength with which he did so aroused her even more. He held her legs and started kissing the soft skin of her inner thighs. Prisha felt like a book whose pages were being flipped very fast. And when she felt him at her vagina, the whole world around her started to reel. She thought the stars above would collapse on her all at once. Her eyes rolled back as he licked faster. She started climbing up the peak of pleasure once again. She thought she would come. And right when she was at the edge, he stopped. Again. She remembered Zinnia's words: someone holding you back right at the top of a roller coaster. But damn! How is he so good at it? Prisha wondered.

Before she could realize that this was perhaps what edging was, she felt his hard penis slowly making its way inside her. He was thick, she was tight. When he was completely inside her, it gave her a pain more precious than pleasure.

Prisha was holding on to his hair with one hand, while the other slowly travelled from his back to his butt. He pinned her hands on either side as he began thrusting. It took her higher and higher and higher still—she was a part of the clouds, the stars, the sky. And yet again, when she thought she would come, he pulled out. It made her feel restless. It was like standing under a cloudy sky. You could almost smell the rain and just when you'd close your eyes to feel the drops hit your face, the clouds would start dispersing.

'I dare you to pull out next time. I want it Saveer. I just want it,' she said. Saveer pulled her up and lay down on his back. She was now on top of him.

'Reach it if you want to,' he said. She was done playing hide and seek. At that moment, she was all about pleasure. She started riding him, at first slowly and then vigorously. She held his hands tight as she galloped towards the first orgasm of her life. And when it happened, a long-drawn-out moan escaped her, her body convulsing. She thought she would never be normal again. Prisha collapsed on his chest. She had come—a toe-curling, stomach-churning orgasm. And so had he. But he had pulled out at the last moment.

'Next time I want it inside,' she whispered, as he cuddled with her.

'We will see,' he whispered back. Neither spoke for a long time.

Prisha kissed his cheeks. 'How did this happen, Saveer? Are we really together?'

'I too want to know the answer. How?' They kissed again.

'Maybe if it were a book, we would have needed a reason. But life, at times, is inexplicable, especially when you fall for someone. Sometimes, I feel the universe is more in control of us than we can possibly imagine. Perhaps you and I were destined to fall in love. How else do we explain this love story of ours to anybody? Or even to ourselves,' he said.

'I have a request,' she said in a half-choked voice and with moist eyes. 'Never leave me. Okay?'

Saveer looked at her for a while and repeated, 'Never leave me too, okay?'

'Tonight you've tattooed yourself on my soul,' she said.

She held him tight and placed her head on his chest. The yacht kept sailing as they lay naked. What neither of them knew was that a woman was standing at the harbour. With tears in her eyes, she was counting the number of days to Saveer's birthday. It wasn't far now. And this time, it was the nineteen-year-old's turn to pay for committing the biggest sin of all: Love.

28

In the morning, the same driver who had dropped off Prisha at the Gateway of India picked them up. Saveer felt hung over after last night. He had finally taken a decision. It was a point of no return. He couldn't afford to lose Prisha. He grasped her hand. She smiled at him and edged closer. He felt relaxed after a long time. There was no similarity between Isha and Prisha and yet the echo of his happiness was still the same.

'I hope I didn't disappoint you?' Prisha said.

'Disappoint?'

'Last night,' Prisha said, blushing.

'I thought you were amazing.'

'Really? I was so nervous. And shy.' She blushed again.

They kept talking as the car made its way through the traffic, towards the airport. It stopped at a traffic signal. Prisha spotted something and her face lit up.

'I'll just come.'

'Listen!'

She was already out. Saveer saw her cross the road and go over to a balloon-*walah* who was carrying heart-shaped balloons. He smiled to himself, glad that she wasn't as old as him. It helped maintain the balance in the relationship. The signal turned green. Saveer asked the driver to park the car and looked out of the window to see if she was done buying the balloons. She had. She pointed towards the balloons while crossing the road. Just then, Saveer saw a truck hurtling down the road, towards Prisha! He yelled at her but by the time she turned her head and saw the truck, it was too late. She was flung high up in the air. Before the body struck the ground, Saveer woke up, shivering.

He couldn't believe that he had been dreaming. He immediately called Prisha. There was no answer. He called her ten times. Same result. He quickly got out of bed, dressed and drove to Prisha's house. The flat was locked. He called Krishna and learnt that neither Prisha nor Gauri and Diggy had shown up to work. He drove to her college. He wasn't allowed to enter the premises since he was neither a guardian nor a parent. He didn't even have any appointment with a faculty member or the dean. Saveer tried to argue but in vain. He drove to the rear side of the college. He parked his car close to the wall, climbed on top of it and then scaled the wall. Once inside, he asked around for directions to the mass communication course class.

Standing at the threshold of the classroom, he took a deep breath, realizing that what he had done was against his nature but he couldn't shake off the sense of foreboding after the ominous dream.

Prisha, along with Gauri and Diggy, were sitting somewhere in the middle of the class, listening to the professor. The professor stopped after noticing the visitor. All eyes turned to Saveer.

'Yes, how can I help you?' the professor asked.

Prisha's jaws dropped on seeing Saveer. She glanced at Gauri and Diggy. They looked clueless as well.

'I need to see Prisha Srivastav.'

'You do? But a class is going on. Do you have permission?'

'I do.' Saveer sounded quite convincing. 'I only need two minutes.'

The professor called Prisha. She stood up and joined Saveer outside the class. The moment she stepped outside and before she could ask anything, Saveer hugged her, tighter than usual.

'I can't afford to lose you,' he said.

It had been two days since they had come back from Mumbai, where they had made love for the first time. It had felt too good to be true. The surprise, the anticipation and then finally the orgasm . . . the night was imprinted on her soul. The way he had kissed her, licked her, touched her—it was as if she had been living inside a house with locked doors and windows for so long and he had suddenly thrown open everything. They had slept naked under the night sky on the yacht. Prisha had woken up to Gauri's call. Saveer was steering the yacht towards the harbour. She couldn't wait to tell Gauri it had finally happened. Although he had gifted her a new dress, Prisha kept the torn one—a memento of the special night.

Ending the phone call, she went and stood next to Saveer. She was at a loss for words. She blushed when their eyes met.

'Where are we?' she asked. It was a dumb question, she knew, but she had to break the silence.

'Don't tell me you've forgotten we are in Mumbai,' Saveer said.

'No, I mean . . . like . . .' she fumbled. But not for long. His mouth was soon on hers and in no time, they were making love, basking in the sunlight. It was short but intense.

They met thrice after coming back to Bengaluru. But seeing him now, here in college, was at once a shocking and a pleasant surprise.

'You won't lose me ever,' she said and added, 'You came here to tell me this?'

'I had a bad dream. I just wanted to see you, hold you,' he said looking into her eyes.

I can cry and smile at the same time looking at you, she thought. And that's when you know how much you can love a person.

'Nothing will be able to snatch me away from you, Saveer. Nothing. And nobody,' she said and gave him a quick hug.

'I'll have to go back to class now. Let's meet in the evening.' The fact that he was there following a nightmare made her feel special. She couldn't wait to share it with Gauri.

In the evening, Prisha took Saveer to 13th Floor Lounge. While he sipped his drink, the music made her feel like shaking a leg.

'Let's dance,' she said.

'But nobody else is dancing,' Saveer pointed out.

'Then let's make a start, baby,' she winked at him. Saveer understood she was already drunk.

Prisha got up and started dancing next to their table. The way he looked at her was more intoxicating than her favourite poison. Her moves became steamier. Saveer suddenly stood up. Prisha thought he would join her but he put his arm around her waist and took her outside. He waited for the elevator and got inside it.

Is he done partying? she thought. She noticed him press the ground floor button. The moment the elevator reached the next floor, Saveer pressed the stop button.

'What's up?' she asked, confused. He tightened his grip on her waist and drew her closer and looked at her intensely. Prisha gulped nervously as she understood his intention of taking her at the moment. He licked the lipstick off her lips. Her entire body stiffened. He unstrapped her dress and sucked on her shoulder till it turned red. Although it hurt her, she didn't utter a word or a moan. Suffering the sexual pain silently was an emotional high, she realized. He kissed her hard on her mouth, smudging the remaining lipstick. Placing his hands on her butt, he picked her up. She responded by wrapping her legs around his waist. He pressed all the buttons with one hand and then pressed *stop* again. The elevator began to move. She somehow managed to break the smooch and said, 'What are you up to, Monster?'

'Let's see if anyone enters at any floor or we smooch till we reach the thirteenth floor again.'

'You are one crazy monster!'

'Now you know,' he said and went after her tongue. The elevator stopped at every floor and every time it did, Prisha's heart beat loudly. The possibility of being caught, Saveer's I-don't-give-a-fuck attitude and her own weakness, added to her arousal. Luckily, nobody entered. However, on the twelfth floor, when the doors opened, a woman saw them kissing. She wanted to barge in but held herself back. She knew she would soon get her time to destroy every spool of what she saw they were busy creating.

Finally, when the elevator door opened on the thirteenth floor, Saveer stopped. They were both gasping for air and looking at each other like two wild animals in heat. It was the longest smooch Prisha had ever had.

'Sorry, I can't dance but I don't lack talent,' he said, slipping into his chair.

'Do I get this whenever I dance?' she asked. He had made her jaws ache.

'Maybe. But do get your make-up right. You look like someone just spoilt you.'

'That someone has spoilt me for life,' she smiled and went to the washroom. Looking at her messed-up self in the mirror, she blushed. In the mess, she felt like she belonged to him. It was a sexy feeling. Revelling in it while she was putting her lipstick back on, she heard someone call her name. It was Zinnia.

'So, someone has grown up fast,' Zinnia said. They hugged. Zinnia eagerly, Prisha formally.

'I'm sorry to have been a little out of touch,' Prisha said.

'A little?' It was a taunt. Prisha knew she deserved it. Except for a few accidental encounters in college, she hadn't met her ever since she moved out of her flat. 'Chuck it. Here with friends?' Zinnia asked.

'Yeah.' Prisha wasn't sure if she should tell her about Saveer. The last time she had mentioned him, she had said she wasn't interested in him. Life had taken a 360-degree turn ever since.

'Same here. Are you done?'

'Yeah.'

'Come, let's go,' Zinnia said.

The moment they stepped out of the washroom, Zinnia spotted Saveer. She paused.

'One second, don't tell me Saveer is your friend now?' she asked, surprised.

'He is.' Prisha gave her a tight smile. Zinnia looked at her and understood that he was more than a friend.

'I just hope you can handle him, sweets.' She sounded sarcastic. It stabbed Prisha.

'Forget about me, even the best had difficulty handling him, if you know what I mean,' she replied and excused herself.

Prisha was quiet during their dinner. It was only when Saveer took her to his place that she spoke.

'Does it matter to you if I say you're not my first?' Prisha said aloud after practising the line in her mind for some time.

'Huh?'

'I had sex for the first time with my ex. Does it matter to you?'

They were sitting close to each other on the couch. Saveer shifted back a little to look at her properly. 'You think I should?'

'Just answer me.'

'No, it doesn't matter to me.'

'Would it matter if I tell you I have fucked several guys?'

'No, it won't.'

'But it matters to me.'

'What does?' Saveer had an inkling.

'The fact that you have fucked so many girls. That they have experienced something through you. You have given them unprecedented orgasms, damn it! And I don't know what to do about it?'

'It's bothering you.'

'You have no idea how much.'

'And you think it is disturbing you because you love me. So, if I love you too then why doesn't it disturb me that someone else was involved with you sexually. Is that it?'

'Maybe when you cross thirty, you stop giving a shit about someone's past. But I'm sorry, at nineteen, it is an issue.'

'Are you suggesting that the difference in our ages is a problem?'

Prisha looked helpless. She came close to him and said, 'What do I have of you that those girls you fucked don't have? Just answer me and I won't bother you with this again.'

Saveer took her hand and kissed it. Her expectant eyes were awaiting an answer. He started unbuttoning his shirt.

'Saveer please . . . Not now,' she pleaded. He didn't stop until he had finished unbuttoning. He stood up.

'Get up,' he said. Before she could, he held her hand and pulled her up. Her eyes were already moist. He hugged her, her face pasted to his bare chest.

'Can you hear it?' Prisha could hear his heart beat.

'None of the other girls have been there. Except for Isha and now . . . you,' he said. Prisha closed her eyes. Tears rolled down her cheeks. Even though he had taken her name after Isha, the one word that had made her desirable, wanted and beautiful was the word *now*. He may not have been her first, but he was *now*. He may have loved Isha once upon a time but *now* his heart beat for her. He may have fucked other women in the past but *now* he only made love to her. For the first time, the power of the word *now* hit her. A relationship lasts as long it's cocooned in the here and *now*. Outside the cocoon, it starts dying.

They sat down on the couch and Saveer placed his head on her lap.

'I apologize because I had to explain it to you. Certain things should be obvious when you are in a relationship. But in the last five years this ...' he caressed her face with his fingertips and continued, 'this is totally unlike me.'

'Don't apologize. I'm glad I made you do something which is unlike you. Who knows, the unlikely may slowly turn into the likely you.'

'If so then you will be responsible.'

'I want to be responsible for everything that you never were but are *now*.' She stressed on the last word. He smiled at her. She caressed his hair gently as Saveer closed his eyes.

She loved the way he calmed her down every time her emotions surged. She even wished he had been a part of her life five years earlier, before Utkarsh. Then she smiled at the thought. Saveer would have been in his twenties but she would have been too young. That would have been weird.

She broke the silence a minute later. 'I want to ask you something else. I don't know if you would answer this or not, but just that it has been with me for some time now,' she said.

'Why did you tell me that you have killed Isha? How did she die? What happened?' Prisha asked and waited for an answer. But all she heard were soft snores. She looked at him. Watching him sleep on her lap while she played with his hair gently, Prisha suddenly felt that she could steer her life. There's a sense of power over life that comes when you know you are inseparable from your loved one. She leaned close to his face. She felt his breath. Inhaling it made her feel one with him. She sat up with her back against the wall and smiled. Slowly, Prisha closed her eyes.

Only Saveer knew he wasn't asleep. He had heard every word Prisha had said but he wasn't ready to answer it yet. Like he hadn't been ready to confess to Isha. And now she was dead.

29

There was a meeting at the G-Punch office where Saveer had called his creative team—including Prisha, Gauri and Diggy. They were supposed to brainstorm for new ideas to make themselves more visible and encourage more women to connect with them. Gauri suggested a G-Punch app which would let people, especially women, not only register themselves but also report any kind of harassment such as marital abuse, with the added feature of writing anonymously if somebody else was being victimized. Saveer loved the idea and announced that he would have a discussion with his accounts team to prepare a budget for the same. They also needed something that would grab attention quickly. Prisha suggested a flash mob.

'We can talk to our batch mates in college to make a group of youngsters wear G-Punch T-shirts and then we can have these flash mobs in malls?'

'I think that's a good idea. We can distribute pamphlets as well after each performance,' Saveer said. Everyone agreed. Saveer entrusted the responsibility to Prisha. She was in charge of creating the group, practising and then performing on the D-Day. Diggy was asked to design the T-shirts. Saveer felt that Diggy would do a good job after Prisha had showed him a few of his sketches. The meeting was dissolved. When Gauri, Prisha and Diggy went to Ishanvi's for lunch, they spotted Sanjeev with his family there.

'Why don't you go say hi to him?' Prisha asked.

'He is with his family!'

'So what? I'm not asking you to hug him or kiss him in front of his wife. Just a hello,' Prisha egged her on realizing Gauri actually wanted to talk to him but was in two minds about it.

'Let me text him first,' Gauri said and sent him a message saying she was in the same restaurant. They saw Sanjeev read the message and then look around for Gauri. When he spotted the three of them, Gauri waved at him. Sanjeev turned his face away, like he didn't know her.

'That was odd,' Diggy said.

'Maybe he is uncomfortable. It's okay,' Gauri said.

Prisha sensed it wasn't as cool as Gauri tried to make it sound. She didn't probe any further. They ordered their food. Once the waiter left, they noticed Sanjeev leaving with his wife and kid. Another waiter was trying to coax them to stay because their order was ready, but Sanjeev seemed adamant. Gauri frowned. She understood he was leaving because of her. But what could she do? She continued eating her food quietly. Then, on an impulse, she stood up. Prisha immediately sensed there would be some problem. Before she could stop her, Gauri had reached Sanjeev.

'Are you leaving because of me?' she asked him. Sanjeev looked at her, then at his wife and then at her again.

'Do I know you?' he said. Hearing that, Gauri lost her cool. She could tolerate his attempts at ignoring her, but the do-I-know-you kind of spinelessness was too much for her to handle.

'You have fucked me with your eyes open so I think you do know me,' she said. Prisha and Diggy had been waiting at their table. They realized it was time for them to get up and join Gauri.

'Excuse me? What kind of nonsense is this?' Sanjeev said loudly. Hot tears of humiliation and anger rolled down Gauri's cheeks. 'I wouldn't have approached you. But what is this? Am I some virus, which will infect you if we are in the same restaurant?'

'Who is this girl?' Sanjeev's wife asked.

'I don't know who she is or what she is talking about. Let's go.' He hurried out with his family, holding the child's hand. Gauri wanted to say something else but Prisha held her hand. She stopped and watched Sanjeev leave with his family. Frustrated, Gauri stamped her foot on the floor and left. Prisha asked Diggy to cancel their order and ran after Gauri.

She caught up with her just as she was about to ride off on Diggy's two-wheeler.

'Gauri, just breathe first,' Prisha said, holding her tight. Gauri buried her face on Prisha's shoulder and started crying.

'Am I so bad that he had to leave the restaurant, Prisha? I don't know what I did to deserve such a filthy treatment. I swear I wouldn't have disturbed his family lunch,' Gauri said between sobs.

'I know you wouldn't have. Calm down now,' Prisha consoled her.

Diggy joined them but he didn't know what to say. Prisha asked Diggy to ride the two-wheeler home while she took a cab along with Gauri. The latter's tears had dried up by then.

'I don't know whether I should say this or not but I think you should end it, Gauri,' Prisha told her at home. 'It's just pointless.'

'I agree,' Diggy added.

'This can't be love Gauri, no matter how much you want it to be.'

'I know this isn't love,' she said. 'Just that I thought it would turn into love one day.'

'Maybe, but for that two people need to be on the same page. There is you who blushed seeing him in the restaurant and there is him who refused to even recognize you. I doubt it can ever turn into love,' Prisha said.

'If it had to then it would've been by now. Just look at Prisha and Saveer. Why don't you learn from them?' Diggy said. For a moment, Prisha felt lucky to have found Saveer. He had come into her life not like a knight in shining armour but as a beast who had to be kissed to be transformed into a prince. Nonetheless, she was happy. At least he was a prince. Not like Sanjeev who would remain a bastard no matter how much or how long you kissed him.

Diggy snatched Gauri's phone and first blocked Sanjeev's number and then deleted it.

'Your phone has been exorcised,' he said, giving it back to her.

'From the time I got to know about this, I also knew it had to come to an end. I am glad it just has,' Prisha said. Someone rang the doorbell. Diggy went to check. He was shocked to see Sanjeev.

'Is Gauri there?' Sanjeev said.

'She doesn't live here anymore,' Diggy said.

'Look I know she is here. I need to talk to her.'

Diggy tried to ward him off but by then Gauri and Prisha had come out. They were equally shocked.

'I don't think it's a good idea to listen to what he has to say,' Prisha almost whispered to Gauri. She walked towards Sanjeev.

'You shouldn't have texted me. It made me nervous. You have to understand. I had told you at the very beginning that I won't let you come between my wife and

I. Didn't I? Our love always was without a destination. You knew it, Gauri. Still, the moment you saw me, you texted. Why? I thought you would approach me next. I just wanted to tell you not to repeat it. If you see me anywhere, pretend that you don't know me. I hope I am clear this time.'

Not even once did he utter the word sorry in his monologue. And that was the problem in their relationship, Gauri thought. It was always her fault.

She smirked. 'What nonsense! Do I even know you? If you come here again, I'll call the police.'

Sanjeev was too dumbfounded to even consider what she had said.

'She means it,' Prisha backed her friend.

'She means it,' Diggy repeated.

'And sorry, she isn't mature enough to handle the kind of love that is without a destination,' Prisha said.

Sanjeev glared at them and even more at Gauri. 'Fair enough, if that's what you want.' He stormed off. Gauri banged the door shut.

'Bravo, girl!' Diggy hugged her. Prisha hugged them both.

'I think I was only waiting for someone else to push me to do it. Sometimes you don't have the courage to save your own self,' Gauri said. No one broke the hug. Just like Gauri needed them, Prisha needed Saveer to save herself from turning into a different person after her break-up with Utkarsh. Finally, she was happy having discovered something she had once pitifully concluded didn't exist: genuine love.

From the next day onwards, Prisha and Gauri got busy coaxing some of her batchmates to participate in the flash mob. She managed to form a group of fifteen students. Prisha let the students rehearse in their flat. Meanwhile, Diggy designed the G-Punch T-shirt.

Prisha called Saveer to see the final rehearsal. He loved it but told her he wouldn't be able to attend the performance the next day because of an important meeting with a client. He wished the participants luck and left early.

The next day, the students gathered at Forum mall at 5 p.m. They were wearing red-and-blue T-shirts designed by Diggy with the G-Punch logo on them. Soon, they started dancing, spreading the message of G-Punch to the people in the mall. A crowd started to form around the group. People were enjoying the performance, recording it and clicking pictures. The flash mob was performing on the ground floor, but even on the floors above, people were leaning out from balconies to watch them.

By the time, the performance ended, Prisha was dizzy with happiness at the response they had gathered. The group quickly distributed the pamphlets, explained what G-Punch was and the work they did. Some enthusiastic men in the crowd came forward to take selfies with the group, to which they obliged.

It was then that Prisha spotted Saveer on the first floor, standing against the railing along with others. She frowned. Didn't he say he had a meeting or had he intended to surprise her? She smiled and called him. Saveer didn't pick up. She looked up at where he was standing; he wasn't there anymore. Prisha excused herself and took the escalator to the first floor. She couldn't see him anywhere. She scanned the area carefully and finally spotted him taking the escalator to the second floor. She wanted to yell out his name but he was too far away to hear her. It was crowded as people tried to make their way downstairs to the flash mob. It was difficult for Prisha to catch up with Saveer as she tried navigating her way through the crowd. By the time she reached the second floor, there was no sign of Saveer. Prisha felt irritated and tried calling him again. No answer. She looked down from the balcony to find that the group was waiting for her. She went downstairs. Once the event was formally over, she thanked everyone, after which the participants left in groups or alone. Gauri and Diggy were waiting for Prisha, who was busy staring at her phone.

'What's up?' Gauri asked.

'I was wondering if I should call Saveer,' she said.

'What's there to wonder? Call him if you want to. In fact, tell him the flash mob was a super success and we deserve a treat.'

Prisha was about to tap on his name to call when her phone rang. It was him. She took the call.

'How did the event go?' he asked.

Really? Prisha thought. *Didn't he see it? Didn't he see me see him?* 'It was a super success,' she said and distanced herself a little from the other two.

'You sound a bit lost. What happened? I'm sorry I couldn't take your calls; I was driving. And then something happened.'

'What?'

'I don't know. For half an hour, I was at the same place even though I was driving.'

'What? I didn't get you.'

'Let me meet and tell you. I'm coming to the mall to pick you up.'

'Okay.' Prisha ended the call and went back to her friends.

'Everything cool?' Gauri asked.

'Yeah. You two go. Saveer will pick me up. I'll join you guys later.'

'Sure. Take care.' They left, scrolling through the selfies they had clicked after the flash mob.

Saveer picked up Prisha in the next ten minutes.

'I'm glad it was a success. Major thanks to you,' he said the moment she sat inside the car.

'What strange thing were you talking about?' she asked.

'Oh that.' He swerved the car out of the mall and on to the road.

'It seems I lost track of time. I was at the same place for fifteen minutes or so.'

'That could be due to the traffic.'

'No. I mean I don't remember it.'

'You don't remember it?' *Like you didn't remember the other day if you had messaged Krishna about the car or where you had dropped the phone? But today I saw you in the mall, damn it!* She thought.

'I know it sounds funny but I actually don't remember,' he said and continued talking about the progress of the G-Punch app. But Prisha was hooked on to the one question in her mind: it was obvious he was there in the mall. So why would he lie? Unless, he was hiding something.

30

Prisha couldn't sleep that night. She wanted to talk to Gauri but she seemed withdrawn after the incident with Sanjeev. She wasn't confident of discussing it with Diggy because his reactions were usually too unnecessarily dramatic and the solutions unrealistic. But the more she kept it to herself, the more claustrophobic she felt.

She thought of asking Saveer directly, but was scared it might adversely affect their relationship. *What could the possible reason for the lie be?* Prisha tried to play the devil's advocate. Sanjeev had lied about Gauri in the restaurant because he was there with his wife and he didn't want the latter to meet the former. What could Saveer's reason be? She couldn't possibly have confused him for someone else, or had she? The man was wearing aviators but could she possibly have confused a random man for Saveer?

The fact that she followed him all over the mall and yet couldn't locate him made her all the more suspicious. Did he intentionally evade her? *But why?* She was back to square one. Her phone suddenly buzzed. It was Saveer.

Didn't call. Maybe you are asleep. If not, then can we please have coffee tomorrow morning at Nandi Hills?

Your wish is my command, she texted back.

Prisha didn't want it to be obvious that she doubted that he had lied to her. Who knows, maybe when he met her the next morning, he would apologize or explain himself. *See you tomorrow at 4 a.m. Will pick you up.*

Sure.

Prisha set an alarm for 3.15 a.m. and tried to sleep. However, she kept tossing and turning in bed and finally woke up a minute before the alarm was about to ring. She got ready and waited for Saveer. At 4.30 a.m., she texted him: *I'm ready, mister. Call when you are here.*

When he didn't arrive by 4.45 a.m., Prisha called him. There was no response. She called him every two minutes and when there was no response even after some twenty calls, her patience ran out. She booked a cab and without waking up either Gauri or Diggy, left for Saveer's house. When she reached, she noticed his bike was not there. She was piqued. She went in and found the main door locked. There was no point ringing the doorbell. Obviously, he was not at home. But where was he? Why wasn't he taking her calls? She called him a few more times but nothing happened. Giving up and not knowing what else to do, she went back to her flat. Once home, she told Diggy about the strange turn of events. He suggested she wait till the evening for him to respond. She waited for the next couple of hours and finally saw Saveer's name flash on her phone screen during one of the lectures in college. She excused herself and got out of class to take the call.

'Where on earth were you?' Prisha couldn't hide the concern in her voice.

'I was . . . I overslept,' Saveer said. He sounded groggy.

'Asleep?' It sounded like a lame excuse to her.

'Yeah and I don't know why I had such a deep sleep.'

'But I came to your house in the morning and it was locked.'

'What?' Saveer sounded genuinely surprised.

'Yes.'

'How can that possibly be? I was at home. In fact, I'm late for office as well.'

'Even your bike wasn't there.'

'Tell me you are kidding.'

'You think I am!' she said and noticed her professor peeping out of the classroom. She understood her pitch was a tad bit too high. 'Listen,' she said, speaking a little softly, 'I'm in college right now. Let's meet in the evening.'

'All right. Come over to my place. I'll clear all the confusion and make up for the missed Nandi Hills trip this morning.'

'Sure, we'll see.'

Prisha ended the call and went back. But she couldn't take her mind off the phone call. What Saveer had told her made no sense. Of course he wasn't in the house, how else would the house be locked? *And I bloody saw the lock. The way I saw him the other day in the mall*, Prisha thought to herself.

Once her classes got over, she went back home.

Just came back from college. I will be there in two hours, she texted Saveer.

I'm waiting, he responded.

Everything is normal and yet, suddenly abnormal, Prisha thought, yawning. But what about the lie? What about the lock? What about Saveer claiming he didn't go out? The lost night's sleep slowly caught up with her and she dozed off for some time. Once up, she immediately left for Saveer's house. She pressed the doorbell. A message popped up on her phone's screen: *There's a key below the doormat*.

She called him immediately. He picked up after the second ring.

'What's up, Saveer?'

'It's a game, which I expect you to play.'

The way he said it, Prisha knew something sexy was coming up. She ended the call and decided to play along. Perhaps it would lead her to something that would clear the air. She found the key under the doormat, unlocked the door and closed it behind her. Inside, she found the house plunged in darkness. The sensors were probably off. She waited for a while to let her eyes adjust to the surrounding darkness.

'Come up,' she heard him say. She looked up to find someone standing at the head of the staircase. The person went back into the bedroom.

'Why aren't the lights on?' she asked.

The figure stopped and said, 'There's only one rule in this game. No questions. Come up now.'

He is really going to make up for the goof-ups, she thought and walked up the stairs and to his bedroom.

'Now what?' she asked, watching Saveer's outline against the window. She saw him typing something on his phone. The screen light was so dim that she couldn't see him properly. Her phone buzzed.

Get rid of your clothes but keep your phone with you.

'Okay,' she said.

This will be really kinky, she thought and removed her top. She unbuttoned her jeans, pulled the zip down and got out of it. Prisha no longer felt shy in front of him. She unhooked her bra and dropped it on the floor, making a small heap of her clothes. Then she tugged her panty down. Another message popped up: *Go to the bed. Lie down. Close your eyes.* She read it with a naughty smile. The bossy undertone of the instructions had an erotic ring to it. Prisha went and lay on the bed. Stark naked. She closed her eyes. And waited for him to do something. It happened in the form of his breath. She felt it on her forehead first. Then it travelled all the way down from her nose, lips, chin, breasts, navel and finally to her vaginal lips. She squirmed a bit holding on to the bedsheet with one hand while tightening her grasp on the phone with the other. He slid down and she felt his breath on her inner thighs. She was covered in goosebumps and she knew she was wet by then.

'You are killing me, Saveer,' she gasped. A few seconds later her phone buzzed again: *Have you ever touched yourself?*

'No,' she answered softly. Her arousal was evident in her voice now.

Place your fingers on top of your vagina and keep me in your mind. Then stroke your clitoris gently.

Prisha did as she was told. Her entire body started shivering as she began pleasuring herself.

'Fuck, I need you, Saveer. Right now. I just need you. Come to me,' she said in short breaths.

An instant later, she felt him blindfolding her.

Did he think I'd open my eyes? She thought and asked, 'Don't you trust me?' she asked. There was no response. She felt him hold her foot and in no time, her right toe was in his mouth. He sucked each one of her toes while Prisha kept squirming on the bed. She could already feel the sexual pleasure reach its zenith. After some time he released her toes.

'Where are you?' she asked and immediately felt his fingers on her wetness.

'No, please. I'll die of pleasure tonight,' she cried. His fingers first started rubbing her clitoris gently and then slipped into her vagina. She was about to say something when she felt his hand covering her mouth and her nose, not letting her breathe. At first, she thought it was accidental and he would remove it. But he didn't. With every passing second, his finger's motion intensified in her vagina. When she knew she was dangerously breathless, Prisha flayed her hands against the bed and tried to push him, but he still didn't release her. For a moment, Prisha thought she would both come and die at the same time. She had indeed come, but she didn't die as he removed his hand. Prisha coughed and gulped huge mouthfuls of air. She had never had such a devastating orgasm before. The one she had experienced in the yacht was romantic but this one was pure evil. She wanted to take her blindfold off.

'I want to drink some water, Saveer. Please let me,' she pleaded. She was given some water but her hands were held tight. She gulped the entire bottle down. Her breath became steady. She realized he wasn't holding her hands anymore. She took off her blindfold but Saveer wasn't in the room.

'Saveer?' Prisha shouted. Her phone buzzed with another message:

You just made love to your death.

Before she could make any sense of it, she felt sleepy and dozed off naked on the bed.

31

I t was Gauri who woke Prisha up, shaking her hard.

'Get up now, will you? We need to go to college,' Prisha heard her say. She sat upright in bed with a start.

'What are you doing here?' she asked.

'What? This is our flat. Where else will I go?' Gauri said and picked up the bowl of cornflakes kept next to the bed.

'I'm in the . . . flat!' Prisha looked incredulous.

'Why are you sounding so shell-shocked? Diggy and I found you in the flat last night.'

'I slept at Saveer's place, that's why I'm shocked. Something's wrong,' Prisha said and stood up. She wore a T-shirt on her spaghetti top and took off her shorts to wear a pair of jeans. While dressing up she remembered she had slept naked the night before. Every thought about last night was giving her a chill.

'Where are you going?' Gauri asked. Prisha didn't say anything. She went downstairs to her landlady who stayed on the ground floor. The old woman always kept an eye on the people coming and going out of the building.

'Hello aunty, I just wanted to ask, did you see the man who dropped me here last night?'

'It was a woman,' the landlady said.

'A woman?'

'Yes. I didn't see her face because it was covered with a dupatta, but it was a woman in a salwar kameez who dropped you off and left.'

For a second, the image of the woman whom Prisha had spotted standing outside her building and staring at her in the darkness flashed in front of her eyes. It made the hair on the back of her neck stand on end. She thanked the landlady and called up Saveer.

'Good morning. I don't know how to say this but I'm sorry I wasn't around last night,' Saveer said. Prisha's hand started shaking. She sat down on the staircase. If Saveer was telling her the truth, who the fuck was she with last night in his house, in his bedroom, on his bed? He had to be kidding.

'Hello? You there?' she heard him say.

'Yeah I am. What were you saying?'

'I said I don't know what happened. I lost track of time again.'

'Could you please check your texts?' she said. While he checked his conversations, she checked hers. She realized she had been mostly replying out loud to the texts that Saveer had sent her. There was nothing in her inbox.

'I don't get it. What should I check? Did you send something?' he asked.

'What's there in your sent item's folder?'

'Nothing. Why?'

That's it. The entire affair had taken a really bizarre turn all of a sudden.

'Let's meet,' she said. That was the best and the only thing she could have suggested.

They met a few hours later at a restaurant for breakfast. She grabbed his phone and checked his sent messages. There was nothing in it.

'Did you delete anything?' she asked.

'No. But you sound like you are sure there was something.'

Prisha was in two minds whether to tell him about what had happened last night. That he had made her masturbate, had blindfolded her and then made her go breathless, while fingering her only to experience a colossal orgasm.

'Hello? Where are you lost?'

'Is there anything you want to share with me, Saveer?' she asked.

There is, Saveer thought to himself, *I'm afraid there is. But what if you leave me after hearing it? What if we never meet again? I didn't involve myself for letting you go. In fact, I simply can't afford to suffer another separation, however justified it may sound after you know the truth. So, I want to tell you a lot but the repercussions may end up murdering this relationship that we've nurtured together.*

'Not really, why do you ask?' he said.

'Just like that.' Prisha wasn't sure how she would describe last night to him. Would it weigh on their relationship? Was he also keeping things to himself and wondering the same? *It's funny*, Prisha thought, *how we try to keep things to ourselves, fearing an adverse effect on our relationships, knowing well that keeping things to ourselves would not have a desirable effect either.*

'Listen, I'm really happy that the flash mob performance was a success. I want to give you three a treat. So, I've booked a table at Molecule tonight. Tell Gauri and Diggy to be there.'

Prisha nodded. Saveer clasped her hand, looked into her eyes and said, 'Lately, I've had this feeling that there has been too much going on. What do you think of you and I going somewhere quieter, away from Bengaluru?' I would really like it. Especially now when I am so confused.

'All right, let's plan tonight after dinner,' he said. She nodded.

Gauri and Diggy were excited to hear about the treat. It was the first time they would join Prisha and Saveer for dinner. Prisha was impressed with the way Gauri had pulled herself out of the emotional mess Sanjeev had put her into after keeping to herself for a few days. But given her history, Prisha knew, she must have handled worse.

Saveer picked them up from their apartment in the evening. He drove them to Molecule. Saveer told the manager that he had a reservation.

'I beg your pardon, sir but you have utilized your reservation a couple of hours ago,' the manager said. Everyone looked at each other.

'I just walked in. There must be some confusion,' Saveer insisted.

'I struck off your name and we do it only after a customer has visited the restaurant. Here it is.'

'Are you saying someone else came, told you that he was Saveer Rathod and you let him have the table?'

'I'm afraid that's how it happens normally. I wouldn't have asked for your identity card but that's not an issue. We have empty tables. I can give you the best one as per your choice.'

'All right, sounds good. What do you guys say?' Saveer asked the other three. Gauri and Diggy had no problem. Prisha's mind was stuck somewhere else. Gauri nudged her and said, 'I'm okay with it.'

They were ushered to the best table available. While the others ate and drank, Prisha excused herself to go to the washroom. But instead she went to the manager. The three at the table assumed she must have been asking for directions to the washroom, but what she wanted to know was where the person who had introduced himself as Saveer had sat. And which waiter had served him. The manager pointed out the waiter.

'Was the person you served at table number fifteen alone?' she asked

'No ma'am, he was with a woman.'

'Could you identify them?'

'I think so.'

'Is the man sitting over there the one whom you had served?' Prisha gestured towards Saveer in the distance. The waiter looked at him and said, 'Seems like it.'

'What do you mean seems like it? Was he or was he not?'

'He was wearing shades. But it seems like him all right. Though I can't be sure.'

Wearing shades? When Prisha had spotted Saveer in the mall, he was wearing shades. Prisha saw Gauri waving at her. She joined the others but spoke less. *Saveer had come to the restaurant but now he was denying it*, she concluded. She had two options, either to confront him and risk everything she thought would be hers, or give it some time.

'Prisha and I are staying back during Diwali. Only Diggy is going home,' Gauri said.

'I'm also going back,' Prisha said.

'But you promised you wouldn't,' Gauri complained.

'I'm sorry, but Mumma insisted so I relented.' By then, Prisha had decided that she didn't want to do anything impulsively, whether it was confronting Saveer or anything else. She needed some time alone to think about the chain of events.

'I think you should go,' Saveer said. *So that you can go to restaurants with random women?* Would Saveer too turn out to be an asshole like Sanjeev? Prisha felt like throwing up at the thought. She still had faith in her choice even though she had been proved wrong earlier. Saveer dropped them home. Prisha said goodbye to him with a formal hug.

The Diwali break proved to be a time for introspection. She took Saveer's calls but didn't call him back. She talked to him but did not initiate a conversation. It was difficult for her but she wanted Saveer to come clean and tell her if there indeed was something. Her instinct said there was but his words, his demeanour told her otherwise. She missed him terribly. Sitting every day in her bedroom, she understood what he had told her once about memories. It was not easy to live with someone's memories. She cried alone because of the intentional non-indulgence but she couldn't help it. A week passed. The Diwali vacation got over. More importantly, Saveer's birthday was coming up. She decided to discuss everything with him. Heart-to-heart. Piling on assumptions in one's heart wouldn't take their relationship anywhere. In fact, it would kill it. Prisha flew down to Bengaluru a day before his birthday. Prisha had a plan. It was, after all, about time they sorted out things between them. Most importantly, opened up their respective emotional closets.

Saveer's Thirty-Fifth Birthday

Prisha's plan was simple. She wanted to give Saveer a surprise the way he had given her on her birthday. She didn't wish him at midnight. In fact, she switched off her phone. If he called, she had told Gauri and Diggy to tell him that she had to go back home due to some emergency. Meanwhile, she had memorized the Kannada phrase, *naanu endendigu ninnavalagirabeku*. She wanted to see his expression when he heard it from her.

The last several weeks had been confusing but she wanted to make sure that they had a fresh start on his birthday. *Second beginnings are important in a relationship*, Prisha thought. It helped inject freshness into stale or sometimes forgotten relationship goals. Once she had given him his surprise, she would talk her heart out to him—everything she had thought, felt and understood, or perhaps misunderstood, about him. The risk of discussing everything on her mind was worth more than keeping things buried inside her and watching herself drift away from the relationship. She would propose to him and then tell him about whatever was troubling her: the night she was blindfolded, the messages and how she couldn't find anything in her inbox the next day. The strange woman who had dropped her home, the fact that she had spotted him in the mall. Saveer's blackouts, his drowsiness. Prisha had a hunch that everything was connected. But to what and to whom . . . she would have to find out.

Prisha got ready and reached Nandi Hills.

Saveer woke up late that day and with a headache. He made a mental note of visiting a doctor since he had been feeling drowsy and dozing off every now and then only to wake up with headaches. The first thing he did was to check his phone. There were no missed calls or messages. He guessed the reason. He called Prisha. There was no answer. He didn't waste time calling her again or waiting for a call. He immediately called Gauri up.

'I don't like surprises on my birthday. I'd told her that before.' Saveer was troubled after he ended the call. Gauri told him that Prisha had gone to Faridabad because of an emergency. All she knew was that Prisha would get in touch with Saveer's assistant to guide him to her—the way he had had on her birthday.

Saveer felt restless. He had a bad feeling about the day, like he usually did on his birthday. In the last five years, he didn't have anyone in his life. But on his thirty-fifth birthday, he had someone around whom his whole world revolved. Just like it had around Isha once. And Saveer knew if Isha's death was the first nail on his emotional coffin, if anything were to happen to Prisha, it would be the last. The doorbell rang. He hoped it was her, but it was his assistant Krishna with a rose and a bag full of chocolates.

'Happy birthday, sir. Prisha ma'am asked me to give this to you.'

'Why didn't you tell me before?' Saveer asked rudely, taking the rose and the chocolates from him.

'She'd asked me to give it you at this time.'

Saveer understood Krishna was innocent.

'Do you know where she is?'

'No.'

'Okay. Thanks.'

There was a note in between the chocolates. It read:

Happy birthday, love. It's an important day for us. Why? Well let's meet where I had met you for the first time as Saveer. Nandi Hills. I'll tell you everything then. I'm waiting. Be quick!

Saveer sighed. At least she was safe. He went for a quick shower. While he soaped his back, he felt an itch around his waist. He switched the lights above the mirror and tried to check. He noticed a reddish tinge on the right side of his waist. He frowned and checked it again on the small magnifying mirror next to the washbasin. Saveer was dumbfounded to find something which resembled a tattoo. It was a word: *happiness. When did that happen?* He wondered and just before he was about to turn, he noticed another tiny tattoo on the left side of his waist. It was another word: *every.* He checked his back in the mirror properly and found two more words in the middle of his back, tattooed in the same way. The words were *fuck* and *your.* It didn't stop there. Two more words were waiting to be discovered right below his shoulders. *I* and *will.* It didn't take him much time to figure out the full sentence: *I will fuck your every happiness.*

Intense fear gripped him as he rushed out of the bathroom to get dressed. Something would surely go wrong today, He was convinced. I hope it is not what I think it is, he panicked.

Prisha was waiting at Nandi Hills for about an hour now. She was sitting right next to the edge of a cliff, muttering the Kannada phrase to herself to perfect it. *Naanu endendigu ninnavalagirabeku. I want to be yours forever.* The place was exactly where she had seen him some nine-ten months ago. If someone had told her this man was going to become her everything in the months to come she would have laughed at that person. But that is what happens. Sometimes, life breaks your expectations in a good way. She never thought a day would come when she would accept her break-up with Utkarsh as a blessing. Patience helps yield perspective. And perspectives, with time, keep changing our definition of what's a bane and what's a boon.

Today was the day of an official proposal. Over the past few months, Prisha had been saving bits of her salary to buy a bracelet for Saveer with *PS* carved on the studded stone. She couldn't wait any longer. She heard some sound at a distance. She turned to see a bike a few feet away. Her heart raced. She had lived this moment in her head so many times that now the anticipation was killing her. She waited for him to come close to her—in her mind, she would turn and simply say the words she had been trying to perfect. And his expression as he tried to comprehend it. Then she would hug him. Kiss him. And tell him that she knows something's wrong but it is okay to share it with her. A shadow fell over her. *He is finally here*, she thought.

'*Naanu endendigu ninnavalagirabeku*, Saveer,' she said out loud and was about to turn around when she heard him say, 'But . . . forever is a lie, Prisha.'

She frowned and turned around only to be blinded by a light being flashed at her point blank.

'I'm sorry,' she heard next and felt a push. It sent Prisha flying off the edge and into the abyss. Her eyes were wide open as she continued to fall. No, it wasn't a dream. And now, Prisha also knew that Saveer had really meant it when he had told her that he'd killed his ex-girlfriend. Before she blacked out, her last thought was: it's too late.

To be continued . . .

Acknowledgments

My heartfelt thanks and deep gratitude to Milee Ashwarya for her continuous faith in my storytelling prowess and fruitful support as a publisher.

My editor Indrani, publicist Shruti and the entire sales team at Penguin Random House for working hard and helping my vision reach the readers smoothly each time.

Deep gratitude to my family for their continuous support and understanding, which allows me to do what I love doing the most.

Anmol, Likhith, Mudita, Lavisha, Paullomy, Harshitha, Ankita and Sharanya: thank you for all your help, support and love.

Special thanks to Sanjana for the late night discussion over LIT; to Anurika, you will know why when you read the book; and to Ranisa, I'm indebted to you for keeping a certain flame alive inside me.

Lastly, the most important person, R. Thank you for holding my universe together.

About the Author

Novoneel Chakraborty is the bestselling author of nine romantic thriller novels. His novel *Forget Me Not, Stranger* debuted as the No. 1 bestseller across India, while the second in the Stranger series, *All Yours, Stranger*, ranked among the top five thriller novels on Amazon, India. His last novel, *Black Suits You*, was among the top five thrillers on Amazon for fifteen weeks straight.

Known for his twists, dark plots and strong female protagonists, Novoneel is referred to as the Sidney Sheldon of India by his readers.

Apart from novels, Novoneel has also written seven TV shows. He lives and works in Mumbai.

You can get in touch with him at:

Email: novosphere@gmail.com
Facebook: officialnbc
Twitter: @novoxeno
Instagram: @novoneelchakraborty
Blog: www.nbconline.blogspot.com

The concluding part of the Forever series

Is it really Saveer who pushed Prisha? Is this what he was scared of ever since he got involved with her? Who is the woman Saveer saw? Who is the man Prisha saw? Is Saveer telling the truth or is he hiding skeletons in his closet? And more importantly, will Prisha survive the fall?

These and all other questions to be answered in the last part of the deliciously twisted two-book Forever series, which is . . .

Coming up . . . real soon!